THE DISAPPEARANCE
OF JOSEF MENGELE

Olivier Guez

Translated from the French
by Georgia de Chamberet

VERSO

London • New York

First published in English by Verso 2022
First published as *La Disparition de Josef Mengele*
© Grasset & Fasquelle 2017
Translation © Georgia de Chamberet 2022

The extracts from *Auschwitz: A Doctor's Eyewitness Account*
by Miklós Nyiszli are taken from the editions published by
Arcade in 1993, translated by Tibère Kremer and Richard
Seaver, republished by Castle Hill Publishers in 2018, translated
by the author, Kladderatasch and Germar Rudolf.

1 3 5 7 9 10 8 6 4 2

Verso
UK: 6 Meard Street, London W1F 0EG
US: 388 Atlantic Avenue, Brooklyn, NY 11217
versobooks.com

Verso is the imprint of New Left Books

ISBN-13: 978-1-78873-588-9
ISBN-13: 978-1-78873-589-6 (UK EBK)
ISBN-13: 978-1-80429-050-7 (US EBK)

British Library Cataloguing in Publication Data
A catalogue record for this book is available from the British Library

Library of Congress Cataloging-in-Publication Data
A catalog record for this book is available from the Library of Congress

Typeset in Electra by Biblichor Ltd, Edinburgh
Printed and bound by CPI Group (UK) Ltd, Croydon CR0 4YY

You who wronged a simple man
Bursting into laughter at the crime . . .

Do not feel safe. The poet remembers.
                                    Czesław Miłosz

The
Disappearance
of Josef Mengele

A NOVEL

Olivier Guez

PART I

The Pasha

Le bonheur n'est que dans ce qui agite, et il n'y a que le crime qui agite; la vertu . . . ne peut jamais conduire au bonheur.

Marquis de Sade

1.

The *North King* cuts through the river's muddy water. Its passengers have been up on deck since dawn, scanning the horizon. As shipyard cranes and harbour warehouses become visible through the mist, some Germans sing a military song, Italians make the sign of the cross, Jews pray. Despite the drizzle, couples kiss. The ship has arrived in Buenos Aires after a three-week crossing.

Helmut Gregor is pensive as he leans against the rail, alone. He'd been hoping that some big shot from the secret police would be there to meet him, enabling him to avoid the hassle of customs. In Genoa, where he embarked, Gregor had begged Kurt to grant him this favour. He'd introduced himself as a scientist, a high-level geneticist, and offered money (Gregor has a lot of money), but the smuggler waved away the bribe with a smile: such privileges were reserved for the biggest fish, for dignitaries of the old regime; there was little chance they would be bestowed on a mere SS captain. Still, Gregor could count on him; he would send a telegram to Buenos Aires.

Kurt took the money, but the secret policeman never showed up. So Gregor waits patiently with the other refugees in the vast Argentinian customs hall. He keeps a tight grip on his two suitcases, a big one and a small one, as he sizes up the nameless European exiles, some elegant, others dishevelled, who stand in long lines. Gregor avoided them during the crossing, preferring to watch the ocean and the stars, or to read German poetry in his cabin. But mostly he spent his time thinking about the past four years of his life since leaving Poland in a panic in January 1945, when he disguised himself as a Wehrmacht soldier to escape the clutches of the Red Army: the few weeks interned in an American POW camp; his release, thanks to false papers in the name of Fritz Ullmann; the three years spent in hiding on a pretty Bavarian farm near his hometown of Günzburg, where – his name changed now to Fritz Hollmann – he cut hay and sorted potatoes; then his escape at Easter, two months ago, crossing the Dolomites via forest paths to arrive in South Tyrol, Italy, where he became Helmut Gregor; and finally Genoa, where Kurt the bandit smoothed his emigration with the Italian and Argentinian authorities.

2.

The fugitive hands an International Red Cross travel document to the customs officer, along with a landing card and an entry visa: Helmut Gregor, height 1.74 metres, green-brown eyes; DOB 6 August 1911, in Termeno, or Tramin in German,

4

municipality of South Tyrol; German citizen of Italian nationality; religion Catholic, profession mechanic; address in Buenos Aires 2460 Arenales Street, Florida district, c/o Gerard Malbranc.

The customs officer inspects the luggage, the meticulously folded clothes, the portrait of a delicate blonde woman, the books and opera records. He pulls a face when he discovers the contents of the smaller case: hypodermic syringes, notebooks and anatomical drawings, blood samples, cell fragments. Odd for a mechanic. He calls the port doctor.

Gregor shudders. He'd taken an insane risk, hanging on to the incriminating briefcase, the precious result of lifelong research, which he had taken with him when leaving hurriedly from his Polish assignment. Had the Soviets arrested him with the case in his possession, he would have been put to death without trial.

Escaping the great German debacle of spring 1945 and heading west, he'd entrusted it to a sympathetic nurse he met in eastern Germany, in the Soviet zone, during a mad expedition after he was liberated from the American camp and spent three weeks on the road. After retrieving it, he passed it on to Hans Sedlmeier, his childhood friend and the confidant of his industrialist father. They'd met regularly in the woods around the farm where he holed up for three years. Gregor would not have left Europe without his briefcase: Sedlmeier gave it back to him before he left Italy, with a big envelope of cash inside. And now a fool with dirty fingernails is doing all he can to turn everything belly up, thinks Gregor as the port doctor inspects the samples

5

and the notes in his cramped gothic script. The doctor, completely baffled, asks questions in Spanish, and the mechanic explains in German that he is an amateur biologist. The two men look at each other, and the doctor, who wants to eat lunch, signals to the customs officer that he can let Gregor through.

On 22 June 1949, Helmut Gregor finds sanctuary in Argentina.

3.

In Genoa, Kurt promised him that a German doctor would be waiting for him at the quayside to take him to Malbranc's house, but once again, it seems, the fixer was telling tall tales. Gregor paces in the rain; his contact is probably stuck in traffic. He scrutinises the wharf, the dockers at work, the families reunited and slipping away together smiling, the piles of leather and bales of wool in the loading bays. No German doctor on the horizon. Gregor consults his watch. The siren of a factory ship wails. He is anxious, hesitant about heading for Malbranc's place, and decides it is prudent to wait. Soon he is one of the last of the *North King*'s passengers left on the quay. Two Calabrians loaded like mules suggest sharing a taxi. Gregor surprises himself by following these fleabags, but on his first day in South America he does not want to be alone, and besides, he has nowhere to go.

4.

At the Hotel Palermo he shares a room, which has neither washbasin nor lavatory, with his companions. They tease him: Gregor from South Tyrol does not speak a word of Italian. He curses his decision to go with them but takes it on the chin, accepts some slices of garlic sausage, and falls asleep, exhausted, his briefcase firmly wedged between his body and the wall, safe from the cupidity of the two men.

Next morning, he gets going. No one answers his phone calls to Malbranc's place. He jumps into a taxi, checking the small suitcase into the left-luggage facility at the train station before heading for a quiet street in the Florida district. Gregor rings the bell of a spacious neocolonial villa. An hour later he returns and rings again, then calls on the phone three more times, without success, from a café where he has taken refuge.

Before Gregor left Genoa, Kurt gave him a second contact in Buenos Aires: Friedrich Schlottmann, a German business-man, owner of a flourishing textile company. In 1947, Schlottmann had financed the covert exfiltration of aircraft manufacturers and Air Force engineers via Scandinavia. 'He is a powerful man,' Kurt said. 'He can help you find a job and new friends.'

Arriving at Sedalana HQ, Gregor demands a meeting with Schlottmann, but is told he is on leave all week. He is insistent, so a secretary takes him to the human resources manager, a German Argentine in a double-breasted suit whose appearance he instantly dislikes. Gregor is surely a candidate for a managerial post, but this young man with slicked-back hair offers him a 'very honourable' workman's job: combing the wool that arrives daily from Patagonia, the standard position for newly arrived allies. Gregor pinches himself; he'd happily throttle the cur. Does he envision Gregor, the son of a good family and a doctor of anthropology and medicine, combing and cleansing sheepskins alongside Indians and dagoes, wreathed in toxic fumes for ten hours a day, in the suburbs of Buenos Aires? Gregor slams the door of the employer's office and swears that when he returns to Europe, he'll skin Kurt alive.

5.

Sipping an orangeade, Gregor takes stock. Get a job; learn one hundred Spanish words every day; track down Malbranc, a former spy in the Operation Bolívar network of the Abwehr, the Nazi counter-intelligence service; try to get along with the two Calabrians he is lodging with even though he can afford a comfortable hotel. They speak only a dialect of the Italian south; he can just make out that they are Fascist veterans of the conquest of Abyssinia. Soldiers will not betray him. Best keep a low profile and hold on to his precious cash. The future is uncertain, and Gregor has never been a risk-taker.

Avellaneda, La Boca, Monserrat, Congreso . . . Staring at an unfolded map, he familiarises himself with the topography of Buenos Aires and feels tiny next to that checkerboard of streets, an insignificant flea, this man who not so long ago terrorised an entire dominion. Gregor thinks of another checkerboard – of huts, gas chambers, crematoria, railways – where he spent his best years as an engineer of the human race: a forbidden city pungent with the stench of burned flesh and hair, surrounded by watchtowers and barbed wire. He moved among the faceless shadows there – on a motorcycle, on a bicycle, in a car – like a tireless cannibal dandy, resplendent in boots, gloves and uniform, his cap tilted rakishly. The prisoners were forbidden to look at him or speak to him; even his SS comrades were afraid of him. On the ramp where the Jews of Europe were selected, his cohorts were drunk but he remained sober, whistling tunes from *Tosca* and smiling. Never did he surrender to a single human feeling. Pity was a form of weakness. With a movement of his switch, he, the all-powerful, sealed the fate of his victims: to the left, instant death in the gas chambers; to the right, a slow death by forced labour or in his laboratory – the largest in the world, which he fed with 'suitable human material' (dwarfs, giants, cripples, twins) each day when the convoys arrived. Injecting, measuring, bleeding; cutting, killing, performing autopsies. A zoo of children was at his disposal, human guinea pigs to help him uncover the secrets of twinship, to produce

9

supermen and increase German fertility so that one day the eastern territories seized from the Slavs could be populated with peasant soldiers, the Nordic race preserved. The guardian of racial purity, the alchemist of the new man, he could look forward to a brilliant academic career and the gratitude of the victorious Reich once the war was over.

Blood and soil, his burning ambition: the grand design of his supreme leader, Heinrich Himmler.

Auschwitz, May 1943 to January 1945.

Gregor is the Angel of Death: Dr Josef Mengele.

6.

His first southern winter: Buenos Aires is enveloped in mist and torrential rain, and Gregor lies in bed, depressed. He has caught a cold. Shivering under the covers, he observes cockroaches racing overhead as they emerge from a ventilation pipe. Not since the autumn of 1944 has he been in such a bad way. The Soviets were advancing across Central Europe; he knew the war was lost and could no longer sleep for nervous exhaustion. His wife, Irene, had got him back up on his feet. Arriving in Auschwitz that summer, she had shown him the first photos of their son Rolf, born a few months earlier, and they had spent some idyllic weeks together. Despite the magnitude of his task – the arrival of 440,000 Hungarian Jews – they had enjoyed a second honeymoon. The gas chambers were working at full capacity; Irene and Josef swam in the Sola. The SS burned men, women and children alive in open-air pits; Irene and Josef picked blueberries, and she made jam. Flames burst from crematorium furnaces; Irene sucked off Josef and Josef fucked Irene. More than 320,000 Hungarian Jews were exterminated in less than eight weeks.

When Josef almost collapsed at the beginning of the autumn, Irene had stood by him. They had moved into a new barracks equipped with a bath and kitchen, with Jehovah's Witnesses as servants.

Gregor looks at Irene's portrait on the bedside table. The photo dates from 1936, the year they met, in Leipzig. He was working at the university hospital; Irene was passing through. She had been studying the history of art in Florence. It was love at first sight for Josef: the young woman was nineteen years old, blonde, with a slender body like a Cranach Venus, his feminine ideal.

Gregor coughs and remembers Irene, in a summer dress, hanging on his arm in Munich's English Garden; Irene blissfully happy in the Opel two-door coupe surging along the Reich's motorways on the day they got married, on the eve of war. Gregor boils with rage as he contemplates for the thousandth time his wife's fine lips in the photo. She refused to follow him to Argentina with their little boy, refused to lead the life of a fugitive across the ocean. Mengele's name is on America's list of war criminals and it has been cited in several trials.

Truth is, she dumped him. Over the years, in the woods and inns around his Bavarian hideout, he could feel the distance between them growing. His friend Sedlmeier, his father and his two brothers, Karl and Alois, told him that, wreathed in black, Irene consoled herself with other men. To 'cover his back', she'd told the American military police he had died in action. 'The bitch', Gregor groans in his hotel attic. Returning from the front, his comrades were welcomed home as heroes by their wives, while his fell in love with a shoe salesman from Freiburg im Breisgau before sending him, Gregor, across the threshold to nowhere.

7.

Upstairs in the bathroom, a towel tied around his waist, Gregor admires his smooth belly, the softness of his skin, his hairless torso. He has always fussed over it. His brothers and Irene mocked his youthful narcissism, the hours spent hydrating and admiring himself, but he blesses the vanity that saved his life. When he joined the SS in 1938, he refused to have his blood group tattooed under an armpit or on his chest to meet regulatory requirements; when the Americans arrested him after the war, he passed for a humble soldier and was released after a few weeks.

Gregor goes up to the mirror and examines the arches of his eyebrows, his slightly prominent forehead, his nose, his malevolent mouth, his face front-on and in profile, and rolls his eyes, which switch suddenly from beguiling to steely and unsettling. This genetic engineer of the Aryan race always wondered about the origins of his mysterious name. 'Mengele' sounded like a kind of Christmas cake or a hairy arachnid. And why were his complexion and hair so swarthy? His schoolmates in Günzburg nicknamed him Beppo the Gypsy. Now, hiding behind a dark moustache in Buenos Aires, he looks like a hidalgo or an Italian: a true Argentine. As he splashes eau de cologne onto himself Gregor smiles and reveals the space between his two upper front teeth. Despite his defeat and the hardships of his escape, and the apparent defection of Malbranc, he's had the strength to fight off his fever. He still has erections. Though thirty-eight years old and harried by life and war, he feels he has not yet lost his power of seduction. Gregor combs back his hair like William Powell in *The Kennel Murder Case*, gets dressed and goes out. The sky is clear, the breeze from the Río de la Plata invigorating.

For some days now he has roamed Buenos Aires. The immense 9 de Julio Avenue and its obelisk; Corrientes, its cabarets and bookshops; the Barolo skyscraper and the art nouveau cafés of the May Avenue; the lawns of the Palermo Parks covered with greasy wrappings; the teeming arteries of the town centre, the patisseries and luxurious boutiques down Florida Street. The day before, he watched the goose-stepping guards in front of Casa Rosada, the presidential palace, struck by the excitement of the onlookers around him and their respect for the military. The army is a stabilising institution in

13

Argentina, as it should be everywhere. Only the Germans strive to destroy their traditions with a collective guilt, he mumbles to himself in the subway on the way back to the rathole where he is staying.

There are pretty women everywhere, flowers, stray dogs, plane trees and gum trees, the smell of cigars and grilled meat, and shops, better stocked than in Europe. Photos of Alfredo di Stéfano in his white-and-red River Plate jersey, and portraits of the tango singers Carlos Gardel and Agustín Magaldi adorn the newspaper kiosks amid engravings of the Virgin and copies of *Sintonía*, the magazine of the stars.

Gregor climbs into a tram and vanishes into the crowds of pedestrians and cars. He does not talk to anyone. The metropolis has welcomed deserters and charlatans ever since it was founded. When he sees red-bearded Jews, the sons of Russian immigrants who fled the tsarist pogroms at the beginning of the century, he switches pavements. He has circled in red on his street map the Villa Crespo district and Once de Septiembre Square, where Jews have set up their garment workshops; he dreads passing a spectre from Auschwitz who might unmask him.

Gregor does not feel out of place. Argentina is the most developed country in Latin America and it is booming. Since the end of the war, a devastated Europe has bought its foodstuffs. Buenos Aires is full of cinemas and theatres; the roofs are grey, the schoolchildren wear uniforms. And just as in Germany in the time of the Reich, the *líder* of the nation is worshipped. A duo, a bear in a military costume from an operetta and a sparrow encased in jewels, the Redeemer and the Oppressed, Juan and Evita Perón, are plastered triumphantly all over the walls of the capital city.

8.

Gregor kills time reading up on their romance in newspapers: they had met in January 1944 at a charity gala for the survivors of the earthquake that had just destroyed San Juan. The young actress Eva Duarte is mesmerised by Colonel Juan Domingo Perón, the strongman among the cabal of colonels in power. He is a spokesman for the voiceless, a sportsman emeritus, a conversationalist, with feline eyes and Amerindian traits. He mobilises the entire country to come to the aid of the devastated city.

After the fundraiser, Perón goes on the radio show where Evita earns a meagre living. At the Ministry of Labour where he pursues his path to power, Evita is hired to work in his department. She is overwhelmed by his passion and generosity. They move in together. Evita makes declarations of loyalty and submission: 'Perón, my sun, my sky, my condor who flies far and high up among the peaks near God. You are my life.'

Perón pursues his plan of action and becomes secretary of war and vice president. He boosts military spending, creates an air force, makes an inflammatory radio broadcast warning of an attack by the Brazilian military, which never happens. At the end of the war, the United States puts pressure on the military junta to hold democratic elections. In September 1945, renewed conservative opposition culminates in a mass demonstration. Argentina roars, rivalries flare between officers, the more liberal ones get rid of the nationalists, and Perón is forced to resign by his opponents in the military. He is arrested. His supporters mobilise and, led by Argentina's General Confederation of Labour, the CGT, they— the workers, unionists and underprivileged—march to May Square in Buenos Aires, and in front of the presidential palace they call for his release and return to power. Perón marries Evita and wins the presidential election a few months later.

Provincial, ambitious and vengeful, Evita and Perón have a lot in common. He is from the desolate steppes of the Chubut region, his father a volatile loser, his mother unfaithful. She is the illegitimate daughter of a bigamous wealthy rancher. In 1911, when the sixteen-year-old Perón joins the military cadets, Evita is not yet born. Posted to Paraná, the Andes, Misiones Province, the young soldier explores Argentina's underbelly and sees peons crushed by overwork, slaughterhouse employees in Buenos Aires more mistreated than the beasts that have their throats cut. Argentina is an affluent country, the main supplier of raw materials to Great Britain, but its wealth comes at a price: the British control the railway network; the Bank of England exploits the riches of the pampas and the vast forests of red quebrachos, which are cut down for use in the tanning industry. The big landowners hold all the power and throw lavish parties. In Buenos Aires there are shacks and mansions in the same street, the Teatro Colón standing close to the brothels of La Boca.

The 1929 stock market crash has a devastating effect on Argentina. Unemployed and homeless people proliferate, strikes paralyse the country, anarchist gangs roam the countryside. Perón contains his impatience with difficulty. Indifferent to the misfortunes of their fellow citizens, corrupt leaders pursue austerity; they advocate democracy but engage in electoral fraud. The 1930s: opium dens, financial scandals, ether and cocaine, armed robbery. In the middle of this infamous decade, a teenage Evita arrives in Buenos Aires to become an actress.

Unscrupulous producers take advantage of the naïve and disempowered young woman. Secretly she seethes: never will she forgive or forget. She dreams of dragging the traitors out of their filthy lairs, of beheading the sugar barons and cattle ranchers connected to those foreign capitalists who trample on her humble kind. Evita is even more fanatical and passionate than Perón.

By 1946, Juan and Eva Perón are the masters of Argentina, backed by the church, the military, the nationalists and the proletariat. The hour of the sword has come.

9.

The Peróns want to liberate Argentina and announce an aesthetic and industrial revolution: a proletarian regime. President Perón thunders and rants on the radio, gesticulates and brags in front of the hypnotised masses, promising the end of humiliation and dependency and a splendiferous life, a new beginning: he is their saviour. Perónist Justicialism will guarantee Argentina a place in the history books.

Perón is the first politician to shake up Argentina's colonial agricultural society. As the secretary of welfare, he spoils the workers; as president, he strengthens public services with the support of the CGT, integrating the national union into the state apparatus. Growth and self-sufficiency, pride and dignity: Perón smashes the privileges of the oligarchy and pursues his dreams of greatness; he centralises and nationalises the railways, the telephone network, all strategic sectors in foreign hands.

Evita is the icon of radical modernisation on the move. The patron saint of the poor receives trade union delegates in evening dress, visits hospitals and factories, opens newly built sections of road, distributes dentures and sewing machines, throws bundles of pesos from the windows of the train on which she indefatigably tours the country. She opens a foundation to help the shirtless ones, and all the underprivileged, and spreads the good Perónist word to cheering crowds. In 1947, during her 'rainbow tour', she is received by Pope Pius XII and several heads of state.

Perónists – mediators between the people and the will of God – nail down the new, nationalist, authoritarian order. They purge universities, the press, the legal and administrative systems, and increase the headcount in the secret service, men in beige raincoats and brown suits. Perón yells, '*Espadrilles*, yes;

books, no!' Dismissed from his position at the National Library in Buenos Aires, Jorge Luis Borges is promoted to the national inspectorate of poultry and rabbits.

Perón's worldview has a transnational perspective. Man is a centaur: half human, half brute, the victim of conflicting desires, galloping through clouds of dust in search of paradise. History is the narrative of the struggle between these human contradictions. Capitalism and communism make an insect of the individual: the first exploits him while the second enslaves him. Only Perónism can move beyond individualism and collectivism. It is a simple and popular creed offering an unprecedented compromise between body and soul, between monastic ideal and supermarket idealism. Perón promises to his people a vertical swing of the pendulum: away from the age of the centaur towards a national, social and Christian Argentina.

10.

Centaurs, the shirtless ones, and the improbable harmony of Perónist antinomies leave Gregor as cold as marble. He is obsessed with getting his bearings and saving his skin.

Spring has arrived in the Southern Hemisphere and Gregor abandons his tourism. In mid-September 1949, he obtains a residence permit and lands a carpentry job in the Vicente

López neighbourhood, where he moves into a new rathole with filthy windows, which he shares with an engineer and his little girl. One night, Gregor is awakened by the moans of the child. Her forehead is burning and her face is pale; her father panics as she is racked with convulsions. He begs Gregor, with whom he has barely exchanged three words, to look for a doctor as soon as possible. Gregor whispers into the engineer's ear that he can cure her, on condition that the man tell no one about his ability. Otherwise Gregor will not lift a finger, the man's daughter will die, and if the man betrays him later, he'll regret it.

No one must know that he is a doctor. The scholar who despised amateurs and manual work as he studied at the best universities in Germany is now building floors and assembling beams. Since the beginning of his escape, he has had to get used to mind-numbing physical work and unsuitable tasks. At the farm in Bavaria, Gregor had to clean out the stable, prune trees, hoe the earth. Here in Buenos Aires, the weeks go by; his life is dreary and solitary. Ever since he arrived he's been fearful of putting a foot wrong, of having an unfortunate encounter. He lives face to face with his fear. He is shackled. Every day, he changes his route to work. He regularly runs across German speakers but dares not approach them. He dreams of a leg of pork and apple juice in one of the German restaurants discovered during his winter wanderings – ABC, in the centre of town, Zur Eiche in Crámer Avenue, or Otto in the Chacarita district – but he resists going inside, unwilling to speak his native language in public. Gregor has a strong Bavarian accent.

To buy *Der Weg*, the monthly mouthpiece of freedom and order, is also out of the question. Gregor consoles himself by picking up his post, still sent to him at the Hotel Palermo. Thanks to his friend Sedlmeier, he stays in touch with Irene and his family: he sends them missives imbued with melancholy via poste restante and Sedlmeier sends in return the letters and directives of his parents. Back home, all is well. The family-run agricultural machinery business is flourishing: the wheelbarrows and combine harvesters are 'selling like hotcakes', his father boasts. Germany has barely cleared up its rubble and is only just beginning to recover. His father, Karl Sr, is waiting for him: as soon as those 'vengeful so-called Yankees stop quibbling' he will return to the family and the board of directors. 'Josef, stop whining, you fought on the Eastern Front, you are no longer a child. You're too mistrustful. Be patient, things will get better.'

11.

Shut away in the room deserted by the engineer and his daughter, Gregor listens to a Strauss opera and devours *Der Weg*. He had a dizzy spell the day before yesterday, dropping his tenon saw and almost falling from a wooden structure several floors high. He owes his life to the agility of the site foreman. Sick of languishing and hoping for the return of the phantom Malbranc, he'd darted to the kiosk to buy the news-paper for nostalgic brownshirts and slipped it under his jacket.

Poems, tortured prose, racist and anti-Semitic articles give the impression that the Third Reich has never fallen. Gregor delights in the Teutonic kitsch of authors silenced by the Allies in Germany since the end of the war. He scours the classifieds on the last pages, discovering fine groceries, breweries, travel agencies, law firms and booksellers – the full extent of the German–Argentinian ethos in the capital – and rejoices: he can leave his bolthole. His life in Buenos Aires can begin at last.

The next day, leaving the building site, Gregor heads for the headquarters of Dürer Publishing, 542 Sarmiento Avenue, to meet Eberhard Fritsch, the director and publisher of *Der Weg*. From behind his desk, Fritsch stares at the Hauptsturmführer Gregor, who runs through his service record without disclosing his true identity: joined the Nazi Party in 1937, the association of Nazi doctors and the SS a year later; military service in Tyrolean Alpine Hunter Corps, volunteered for the Waffen SS, medical expert in SS Race and Resettlement Main Office in occupied Poland; medical officer with SS Division 'Wiking' on the Eastern Front after the beginning of Operation Barbarossa; posted to the Ukraine; took part in offensive in the Caucasus, in action near Rostov-on-Don and at Siege of Bataysk; awarded Iron Cross First Class. Gregor proudly details to Fritsch how he rescued two tank crewmen from their burning vehicle. He mentions his transfer to a prison camp in Poland, but not Auschwitz per se, and bewails his fate, his exile and the occu-pation of his beloved homeland. He deplores the vastness of

Buenos Aires and expresses his nostalgia for the uniform. He needs to unburden himself.

Fritsch lights a cigarette and sympathises. He retains a dazzling memory of the Hitler Youth rallies in which he took part, at age fourteen, during his only visit to Germany, in 1935. He does not believe a word of the horrors that Allied propaganda imputes to Nazism – 'lies made up by the Jews'. He founded Dürer Publishing in order to help out soldiers like Gregor. He offers a voice through his newspaper columns to the 'Blood and Soil' literati who are censored in Europe; he also sees that they get special offers in times of scarcity – stock cubes, tinned meat and cocoa powder. To the comrades stranded on the banks of the Río de la Plata, he offers a rallying point and access to networks. Young Fritsch assures Gregor that he has 'a very long arm' and can guarantee the older man has nothing to fear: in Argentina, land of fugitives and as large as India, the past does not exist. No one will ask where he comes from or why he is here. 'Argentines do not care about European bickering, and they resent the Jews for having crucified Christ.'

Gregor listens to a radiant Fritsch telling him about the party held in Luna Park stadium in Buenos Aires celebrating the Anschluss; how an officially neutral Argentina was the bridgehead of Nazi Germany in South America during the war. The Germans laundered millions and millions of dollars there and bought foreign currency and raw materials. Their intelligence services set up regional headquarters in Buenos Aires. 'The overthrow of the pro-American Bolivian government was organised here, in late 1943,' he says. 'Perón and the colonels, who took power that year, were seeking a way to join forces with the Führer. They beat up marchers celebrating the liberation of Paris and blocked the distribution of Chaplin's film, *The Great Dictator*. When Berlin fell, Perón banned radio stations from transmitting the news: we wanted to build an axis of pro-Nazi nations to fuck over the Yanks. But they forced us to sever diplomatic relations with Hitler, then to declare war on Germany. We resisted with all our might until the end of winter 1945. Argentina was the last nation to enter the war . . .' The phone rings. Fritsch stops short, and dismisses Gregor.

12.

He'd happily punch that pretty boy with grey-blue eyes in the mouth. Or land a good hammer blow on his fingers. Wham! Right on the knuckles, or else on the nails; yes, he would gladly tear the nails from each of Fritsch's hands, strip them off the fingers one by one. Gregor mimes the scene in the bathroom of his Vicente López rathole, mumbling, 'How dare you, Eberhard, you little Argentinian shitbag! Just two weeks in Germany and you lecture me from the lofty heights of your twenty-eight years? Ah, yes, the 'horrors', as you put it, the horrors were real enough, a besieged Germany had to defend itself, crush the forces of destruction by any means. War is not child's play, and Nazism, you dreary moron, does not end with

24

Hitler Youth's grandiose choreography.' Gregor crushes his tube of toothpaste and calms down, abruptly, fearful he will be late getting to the building site. He finds even a slight delay intolerable.

Gregor visits the journal more and more often; it is a Nazi hub in Buenos Aires. He bumps into a thug he had heard about in Auschwitz, one of his regular suppliers, accompanied by a dog trained to shred human flesh. Josef Schwammberger was a commandant of forced labour camps and liquidated several ghettos in Poland. It is here, also, that Gregor meets Reinhard Kopps, the Judeo-Masonic conspiracy specialist for the newspaper, formerly with Himmler's intelligence agencies in the Balkans, and he befriends too the man whom Fritsch considers to be his 'best wordsmith, the great craftsman behind the growing success of Der Weg'. Gregor has already spotted Willem Sassen's well-constructed articles. Although he's knocking back the whisky and chain-smoking (Gregor does not smoke), the Dutch polyglot in a pinstripe suit makes a good impression. Gregor has always taken care to cultivate influential individuals and mandarins: both at university and at Auschwitz, he never mixed with the SS rank and file, just the chiefs and camp commandants. He cannot bear mediocrity.

The two men sniff at each other. Like Gregor, Sassen volunteered for the SS, fighting in a Dutch squadron on the Russian front that advanced into Soviet territory and the Caucasus, where he was badly injured. Also like Gregor, Sassen – a Third Reich propagandist on Belgian radio, and a high-level collaborator – was arrested after the war. He was sentenced to years in a Dutch prison, but escaped twice before finally reaching Ireland. From there, he sailed a schooner to Argentina.

Sassen appreciates his new friend's classical culture as well as the strength of his convictions. Gregor trusts his discretion, and for the first time since arriving in Buenos Aires, he reveals his true identity and history. Like all the others – women to begin with and then Fritsch, who pays Sassen a fair salary and his rent – Gregor is seduced by Sassen's imposing bearing and loquaciousness: in just a few months, the shrewd Dutchman learnt Spanish to perfection and carved out a niche for himself in Argentina. Gregor is impressed by his address book. Sassen will introduce him to Rudel as soon as he can, since he is his occasional driver and ghost-writer. Colonel Hans-Ulrich Rudel, famous ace of the Luftwaffe, the most decorated pilot in German history (2,530 missions, 532 tanks destroyed), is also a refugee in Argentina. Along with several other VIPs, Gregor will also meet President Perón, who 'always has lots of time for the Germans'.

13.

Perón reveres those officers of the great German state who taught him the art of military command at a time when the Argentinian army wore spiked helmets and was equipped with Mauser rifles and Krupp cannons. Panache, authority, discipline; young Perón is so fascinated by German military engineering that he writes a thesis on the first battle of the Masurian Lakes and rarely falls asleep without reading his favourite Prussian strategists – Clausewitz, Count Alfred von Schlieffen and Colmar von der Goltz, the 'nation in arms' theorist whose model of society Perón is trying to impose on Argentina now that he has seized power. All of his national strategies are subordinate to the objectives of his national defence policy.

He is enthralled by the Kaiser's Germany, and then by Italy after Mussolini's rise to power in the early 1920s. Like all the lasso-throwers of his generation, Perón is dazzled by the exploits of Italo Balbo and Francesco di Pinedo, those flying Fascists; intrepid airmen who circumnavigate the starry ether connecting Rome to South America. Perón listens to the voice of il Duce broadcasting on the Argentinian airwaves and hurries to the Palace picture house to watch *One Man, One People*. Mussolini impresses him: a leader guided by the hand of Providence who can save a nation and break the continuum of history.

He explores Italy in 1939 after studying Mussolini's theories of Fascism and war, and serves as a military attaché at the Argentinian embassy in Rome. For two years he travels, educates himself and makes notes; Perón is convinced that he is at the heart of a historical experience not seen since the French Revolution: the founding of a genuine populist democracy. Mussolini has managed to unite scattered forces to focus on the objective he laid out: national socialism. On 10 June 1940, the Italian Army goes to war. From the balcony overlooking Piazza Venezia, il Duce in ceremonial uniform titillates a huge crowd as Perón looks on.

A few months earlier, Perón travelled to Berlin and on to the Eastern Front, after the surprise invasion of Poland. He read *Mein Kampf* in Italian and Spanish and admired the bronze sculptures of Breker and Thorak. Perón is amazed by all the changes: Germany is rising once again with Nazism healing its wounds; no other country in Europe is such a precisely calibrated, well-oiled machine. Germans work in an orderly manner, serving a perfectly organised state. A volcanic Hitler hypnotises the masses: History is dramatised, the will triumphs in movies like *Storm over Mont Blanc* and *The White Ecstasy*, films with Leni Riefenstahl, which Perón discovers during his German pilgrimage; in them death and courage go hand in hand. The Hitlerite lava flow is set to destroy everything in its path.

Back in Argentina, Perón formulates a vision based on a personal narrative of the war that is raging. Fascist Italy and Nazi Germany offer an alternative to communism and capitalism, so the United States and the USSR are allied in their fight against the emergence of this third force, the Axis, the first block of nonaligned powers, according to Perón.

When Germany and Italy are defeated, Perón is determined Argentina will take their place, sure he will succeed where Mussolini and Hitler have failed; the Soviets and Americans will destroy each other soon enough with atomic bombs. The resolute winner of the Third World War may be antipodean:

Argentina has a great card to play. While he waits for the Cold War to unravel, Perón becomes the ultimate rag-and-bone man. He scours the garbage cans of Europe, carrying out a gigantic recycling operation: he will dominate History with the detritus of History.

Perón opens the borders of his homeland and welcomes thousands upon thousands of Nazis, Fascists and collaborators: soldiers, engineers, scientists, technicians and doctors. War criminals are invited to build dams, missiles and nuclear power plants, turning Argentina into a superpower.

14.

Perón personally oversees the smooth running of the Great Escape. He creates a special department based in Buenos Aires: the Information Office, headed by Rudi Freude, son of the main backer of his victorious presidential election of 1946, Ludwig Freude, a wealthy Nazi banker and shareholder in Dürer Publishing. Perón dispatches a blue-eyed crook, the former SS captain Carlos Fuldner, to Franco's Spain, then Switzerland and finally Rome and Genoa, where Gregor embarked. Freude and Fuldner are responsible for a system of escape routes, the 'ratlines' – coordinated expatriation networks, complex chains of diplomats and corrupt officials, spooks and clergymen who offer absolution to war criminals as a stay of proceedings. The final, all-out battle against atheistic communism gets under way.

Buenos Aires in the late 1940s becomes the capital of the rejects of the fallen Black Order. A melting pot of Nazis, Ustashe Croatian counter-revolutionaries, Serbian ultra-nationalists, Italian Fascists, Hungarian Arrow Cross Party members, Romania's Iron Guard legionnaires, Vichy French, Belgian Rexists, Spanish Falangists, fundamentalist Catholics; killers, torturers and adventurers: a ghostly Fourth Reich.

Perón chooses his desperadoes. In July 1949, he extends amnesty to all those who entered under a false identity and sometimes receives them at Casa Rosada.

One balmy, moonless night in December, as Jacob's ladders clink and a breeze ruffles the water, Gregor follows Sassen down a quay running alongside some pleasure boats. The two men whisper 'Centaur' into the ear of a thug who frisks them thoroughly, backed up by three accomplices of a similar stocky build. The Dutchman and the German climb onto the deck of the *Falken* and enter the smoky fo'c'sle amid a hubbub of Central European and Hispanic chatter.

Sassen eagerly takes the glass of beer handed to him by a plump woman; Gregor just has water. 'You're lucky,' murmurs Sassen, 'there's top brass here tonight.' He indicates a man hiding behind a pointed goatee and dark glasses rimmed with black metal: 'Ante Pavelić, the Croatian *poglavnik*' (850,000 Gypsy, Serbian and Jewish victims). The man is surrounded by a wall of Ustashe. Sassen also points out Simon Sabiani, former 'mayor' of Marseille, sentenced to death in absentia in France, and his friends from the Parti Populaire Français; Vittorio Mussolini, second son of il Duce, with Carlo Scorza, former secretary of the national Fascist Party; Robert Pincemin, who led the militia in Ariège; Eduard Roschmann, the Butcher of Riga (30,000 Latvian Jews murdered), 'squiffy as usual'; and the physicist Ronald Richter, the president's pet who has promised Perón he will be the first to succeed at nuclear fusion. An island on a Patagonian lake has been put at his disposal so he can continue his research, Sassen tells Gregor. And Col. Rudel, it seems, is on his way.

Gregor knows no one there other than Kopps, Schwamm-berger and the tough guy in golfing plus fours, who are having a discussion in front of a porthole. Surprise, surprise, this is the lawyer Gerhard Bohne, administrative director of the T4 'euthanasia' programme (2 million sterilised, 70,000 disabled gassed), whom he met several times in Auschwitz. He goes to greet them as they fall silent. Four men climb onto an improv-ised platform: an Argentine colonel, Fuldner and Freude Jr, 'our guardian angels', and a forty-year-old in a three-piece suit and bow tie. 'The Belgian queer', says Sassen, smiling, 'Mr Pierre Daye.' Daye begins to speak.

A few months ago, Daye helped to establish the National Socialist Centre in Buenos Aires: a group of Rexists, Fascists and Ustashe, they aimed to crush American capitalism and Russian Bolshevism, and agitated for amnesty for 'Christian' war criminals imprisoned in Europe. On the eve of the Third World War, the continent cannot be without such high-ranking fighters.

Daye alludes to the original Fall, the murder of Abel by Cain, and the eternal fratricidal struggle that has poisoned human society since Creation. 'Contemptible cosmopolitan materialism and with it the negation of God, this is the enemy and the cause of all our misfortunes!' thunders the fervent Catholic. 'We must bring together our families and carry on fighting. Nothing and no one will stop our triumphant march towards the reconciliation of Nazism with Christianity . . .' The audience whistles and applauds, Daye jubilates and continues in a nasal tone: 'Magnificent President Perón, to whom we owe our freedom, has made this fraternisation his mission. We will help Argentina become the hemispheric counterweight to the United States. It is time to begin, dear friends. The Russians and Americans will fight each other to the death. Over the past year, the Berlin blockade nearly collapsed. Today, tensions are multiplying around the world. So let us be patient, the future is ours, we will return to Europe . . .'

Sassen grabs Gregor's arm and asks him to go up on deck, as he has 'two dear friends' to introduce to him.

'*Oberst* Rudel,' mumbles a thickset shadow.

'Malbranc,' whispers a more graceful one.

Gerard Malbranc, at last.

15.

There are times when Gregor still dreams of boarding a steamer leaving for Hamburg, loaded with a cargo of red corn and purple linen, bringing him closer to Irene. On the third Sunday of Advent, sitting at a bistro table in the harbour, he wrote a letter to her very unlike his other missives. Never before had he declared his passionate feelings for her with such ardour, never before had he expressed such regret for being so far away. He rehashed his memories of their time together: a thousand nights of love; a luxurious summer in Auschwitz; Christmases snuggled up and cosy on his return from the front; the last day, in the snowy woods, snowflakes glistening in her golden hair, when, once again, he asked her to join him, begging her once again to cross the Atlantic. In return, Irene sent a photo of Rolf in lederhosen, primly wished him a happy new year for 1950, and advised him to buy a dog to lighten his solitude. Bizarrely, he hurried to do her bidding, and was offered a pooch he named Heinrich Lyons. Irene suggested Henry Lyons – the name of an American relative – but Gregor Germanised it. What a find! Henry the Lion, the name of the founder of Munich, a powerful prince, Duke of Bavaria and Saxony, and now of Gregor's dog.

He receives good news from Germany: the death, at Christmas, of his younger brother, Karl Thaddeus. Gregor, the

33

elder by just sixteen months, had always hated Karl in an abstruse way. He struts about the sunny terrace of a Florida Este brewery as he remembers their childhood in the big house with narrow windows like embrasures. Karl had once stolen his mechanical train. When their mother got home the little boy had whined and the big boy had been punished. The authoritarian Walburga Mengele had beaten Josef and locked him in the cellar. Karl was always given more generous portions at suppertime. Karl went with their mother to the pastry shops in the Marktplatz. The little shitbag. 'Beppo', as Gregor was nicknamed, had prayed for his brother's death in a fire or in a car crash a thousand times over. He had chewed over his jealousy as he threw pebbles into the Danube running through Günzburg and its woods. Now Karl has joined Walburga in the crematorium.

In the letter announcing the death of his brother, his father also tells him that the Allies are 'getting more reasonable'. Over recent months, prosecutions for war crimes have been suspended and former Nazis have been allowed to take up important positions in the government and industries of the Federal Republic. 'They are beginning to understand who their real enemies are. The Cold War is opening their eyes. And we, Josef, we must forget the war. We are working on reconstruction and moving on. We'll see how that old fool Adenauer gets things moving.'

Gregor is lazing about in Florida Este because he has just moved into Malbranc's place. They have seen each other often, after meeting on board the *Falken*. Malbranc is profusely apologetic: he travels a great deal for his business. When he's in Buenos Aires, he tends to spend more time in his residence at Olivos than the one in Florida, since his wife prefers it. Gregor was unlucky; he dropped by and telephoned at a bad time. When Malbranc suggests that he move in, Gregor jumps at the chance. His sad suburb is left well behind him for the stunning villa, a cosy bed, a luminous airy room soothed by the patio fountain, bread rolls, eggs and a good Austrian cook who works night and day in the kitchen.

He cherishes his host, Malbranc. A former Nazi spy who hid radio transmitters and was an arms dealer during the war, he is a pillar of Nazi society in Buenos Aires. Regular visitors include Karl Klingenfuss, former senior diplomat in the Jewish Department of the Ministry of Foreign Affairs; the great Bubi (Ludolf von Alvensleben), sentenced to death in absentia in Poland, Himmler's personal adjutant officer and a friend of Herbert von Karajan; and Constantin von Neurath, the son of Hitler's foreign minister. Fritsch and Sassen come to play poker, accompanied by an architect who is passionate about music and German classical literature: Frederico Haase. He wears a carnation in his buttonhole and falls for Gregor.

By covert means and underground ways, Gregor had managed to navigate the *porteño* labyrinth.

16.

Perón proclaims 1950 Year of the *Libertador*. El Líder poses as the heir of Gen. San Martín, father of Argentinian independence.

On 25 June, the Korean War breaks out. On 14 July, Adolf Eichmann arrives in Buenos Aires under the pseudonym Ricardo Klement. He doesn't stay long. Fuldner finds him a job at Capri, a public company that builds hydroelectric plants in Tucumán Province.

17.

Of all his new allies, 'Uli' Rudel is Gregor's favourite. Shot down thirty-two times, the eagle of the Eastern Front had always managed to get back to the German lines even though Stalin put a price of 100,000 rubles on his head – a fortune. Hit by an anti-aircraft shell, he had his leg amputated below the knee. Two months after the operation, in February 1945, Rudel got back into his Stuka and amid screaming sirens blew up twenty-six Soviet tanks before surrendering to the Allies on 8 May 1945.

When the airman shows him the Knight's Cross – the Iron Cross with golden oak leaves, swords and diamonds awarded to him alone, by Hitler in person – Gregor looks at him with childlike wonder: Rudel truly belongs to the patrician master race. He plays tennis despite his prosthesis, and has just climbed Aconcagua, the highest peak in the Americas.

Rudel is a descendant of the Teutonic Knights. When he was sixteen or seventeen, Beppo Mengele had embellished their legends in tales told in front of the campfire during celebrations of the summer solstice, when he was running the local branch of the nationalist and conservative youth movement, the Grossdeutsche Jugendbund. Rudel is a German warrior, such as Gregor considers himself to be and as Rudel seems to consider him in turn, despite his lowly rank: 'Gregor' is just a minor SS captain, after all. The colonel enjoys meeting him at the ABC Restaurant when he is passing through town.

Whenever they get together the two Nazis talk for a long time. Neither of them drinks alcohol. They both theorise by means of arithmetical logic and share the same romantic disappointments – Rudel's wife filed for divorce before he left for Argentina. They also share the same apocalyptic vision of the 'degenerate', 'amoral' Weimar Republic of their youth; the same conviction that Germany was stabbed in the back in 1918; the same 'total' devotion to the German people and German bloodlines. A struggle, everything is a struggle: survival of the fittest is the Aryan law of nature; the weak and the undeserving must be eliminated. Purged and disciplined, Germany is the greatest power in the world.

Sitting down with the heroic pilot, Gregor aggrandises his own past as a soldier of biology and hides nothing. Mengele removes Gregor's mask. As a doctor, he cared for the master race and protected the community of fighters. In Auschwitz he fought against racial degradation and domestic enemies, homosexuals and asocials; against the Jews, those microbes that had worked through the millennia to undermine Nordic purity: they had to be eradicated, by any means. He did so out of moral duty. Using all his strength in the service of purity and the promotion of the creative powers of Aryan blood, he fulfilled his duty as a member of the SS.

Gregor is fascinated by Rudel because of his tremendous success. An adviser to Perón, he is spearheading the development of the first South American jet fighter, the Pulqui II, alongside the brilliant aircraft designer Kurt Tank, another German expatriate. He is earning a fortune as an intermediary between Argentina's air force and several German industrial giants – Daimler-Benz; Siemens-Dornier, for seaplanes – thanks to the import licences which Perón generously grants him. Free to come and go as he pleases, Rudel travels from Europe to South America, from one scene of operations to the next. He is at the heart of all intrigues and behind the Odessa and the Spider and Lock Gates escape networks. Rudel is co-founder with von Neurath of the 'Kameradenwerk' relief organisation, sending parcels to friends imprisoned back home and paying their legal fees. He is the commander of Nazi emigration. Rudel takes Gregor under his wing and warns him: forget the Nazi treasure, make no mention of it to anyone, ever.

Crazy rumours are circulating in Buenos Aires regarding this treasure. Shortly before the end of the war, Martin Bormann, Hitler's private secretary, reportedly sent planes and submarines to Argentina packed with gold, jewels and works of art stolen from Jews, in what was known as Operation Tierra del Fuego. Rudel would have been one of the carriers of the booty, which was placed in multiple accounts in the name of Eva Duarte. After their marriage, Perón would have got his hands on the Nazi gold, enabling his wife to finance her foundation. Just recently, the bodies of two bankers suspected of handling the loot were found in the streets of Buenos Aires. 'Otherwise everything is possible in Argentina,' says Rudel. 'Gregor, do you know my motto? You only lose if you give up.'

18.

So Gregor frees himself. His father and Sedlmeier continue to support him, and they agree to his fronting the family business in Argentina in order to explore the vast market for agricultural machinery on the American subcontinent. He is encouraged by Rudel, who flies him to Paraguay to extend his research: the country is home to various German farming colonies, one of the oldest being 'Nueva Germania', which was founded by Elisabeth Nietzsche, the philosopher's sister and a fanatical anti-Semite. The southeast abounds in fertile meadows, and there is a need for everything from wheelbarrows to combine harvesters; Mengele manure-spreaders and fertilisers would be particularly prized. And the region is safe. Rudel has numerous friends in Villarrica, where the first Nazi party outside Germany was founded in 1927.

Sassen does not forget his doctor friend. He occasionally sends deals his way, which are of a more sensitive, albeit lucrative, kind and well matched to his skills. Young, well-heeled women who have been led astray are given a helping hand. Instead of being born in some distant city and abandoned in an orphanage, the fruits of their sins can be exterminated in Buenos Aires by the good doctor. Abortion is a crime that is severely punished in Catholic Argentina, but Gregor accepts the work. He has retrieved his briefcase of samples and medical instruments (scalpels, blades, pliers) since moving into Malbranc's place. How could he possibly refuse to rescue such respectable families? His hands twitch. At last, he can return to medical practice after so many years working as a labourer and farmer.

At the end of 1950, the fascists of Buenos Aires are euphoric. The Third World War is within reach; Perón monitors telexes, his finger on the trigger. Tensions are mounting in Korea. President Truman promises to use America's entire arsenal of weaponry to counter the North Korean offensive in the South. General MacArthur wants to construct a belt of radioactive cobalt stretching between the Yellow Sea and the Sea of Japan to block the Chinese and Soviets from entering the combat zone.

As they wait for Perón's imperial dreams to materialise, Gregor and his new friends lead a highfalutin life. Haase and

Gregor, their hair lacquered to match their highly polished ankle boots, attend performances of Wagner's *Tristan* and Bizet's *Carmen* at the Teatro Colón, according to Clemenceau the world's most beautiful theatre. The music-loving architect and doctor dine at Café Tortoni, or at Hotel Castelar, and between mouthfuls of the highest-quality steak wax lyrical about the sublime nature of German music, which encompasses all the senses and soars to infinity. Sassen has a soft spot for Mexican variety shows, and sometimes takes his friend along with Fritsch to the Fantasio cabaret in Olivos, his favourite dance club, frequented by producers and actresses. Each plays a role: Fritsch pays, Gregor ogles the sirens with their long Indian tresses, Sassen drinks, dances and fondles the *yeguas* (voluptuous slutty mares) and *potrancas* (wild young fillies), leaving his wife and daughters to languish at home. Twice a week, on Wednesday and Saturday, Gregor visits a *lechera*, an expert cocksucker, in a shady club on Corrientes – yet another of Sassen's suggestions. Gregor does not allow any of these docile girls to touch his skin: just his cock, and no kissing or intimacy either. He pays, ejaculates and leaves.

When it's too hot in Buenos Aires, they spend weekends in the pampas, at Dieter Menge's place. A former pilot who made his fortune recycling scrap metal, he is another of Rudel's buddies. His large *estancia* is surrounded by eucalyptus and acacia trees. A bust of Hitler brightens up the garden, and a swastika in granite adorns the bottom of the swimming pool. The evenings are long, the air is clear, and the men bond with one another as brothers in arms over their military exploits,

41

united in swapping convictions. The Nazis drink beer and schnapps in their shirtsleeves, grill great chunks of beef and suckling pig, belch and talk about their faraway homeland and the war. Gregor is not talkative, but Sassen excels at this little game, animatedly imitating crashing shells and wailing missiles, bombardments, recalling the blackened faces and the ragged uniforms of Stalin's Siberian divisions. Every 20 April, Menge and his gang organise a torchlight procession to honour the Führer's birthday. Rudel sometimes takes a newcomer on a trip to this promised land. On one occasion it is Wilfred von Oven, a former close collaborator of Goebbels; on another, a prestigious visitor passing through, the scarred SS commando Lt-Col. Otto Skorzeny, who, high on methamphetamines, swooped in on a glider to rescue Mussolini when he was under house arrest in Abruzzo after the Allied landings in southern Italy. Reinvented as an arms dealer, Skorzeny claims to have seduced Evita during the Spanish stage of her rainbow tour; 'Bang-bang, what a sacred slut the señora Perón is!' he trumpets. Fritsch sniggers while Sassen toasts the Reich and Argentina, where life is good for the Nazis.

In mid-March 1951, Menge invites the whole wild horde to the estancia. Rudel, Malbranc, Fritsch, Bohne, Sassen, Haase, all come to celebrate their buddy Gregor's fortieth birthday. They have a gift for him: an engraving by the stupendous Albrecht Dürer: *Knight, Death and the Devil.*

19.

MacArthur is relieved of his command in the Far East, and the front stabilises. Perón rages as the dawning of the age of the centaur and the Third World War are postponed. His grandiose ambitions thwarted, he turns his attention towards a triumphant re-election. The regime is strengthened: defamation of the authorities is prohibited and the national broadsheets are censored; *La Prensa* is closed, expropriated and transformed into an instrument for the CGT. Military personnel doubles; propaganda intensifies; dissidents are thrown into prison; parliamentarians take refuge in Montevideo. Perón enlists the Lady of Hope to help him win the greatest of victories: he offers the vice presidency to his wife.

Huge crowds greet Evita every day at the Ministry of Labour and outside the headquarters of her foundation, whose budget has increased tenfold. People fight to exchange a few words with her or just to glimpse her as she passes. To touch her hand is to touch Christ. She is the most generous of goddesses: Evita gives houses, medicine and clothes to the poor, and makes myriad sacrifices, as though her days were numbered. She barely sleeps, working long hours on all fronts, as if the regime were under threat. She hides weapons and makes plans to create a private militia of workers in her pay.

Her image is on campaign posters all over Buenos Aires. Immense banners hang from the obelisk on 9 de Julio Avenue calling on people to vote for 'Perón – Eva Perón the icon of the homeland'.

On 22 August 1951, hundreds of thousands of Argentines, the Perónist emblem on the back of their jackets, converge on the widest avenue in the world, where the spouses must officially announce their candidacy. Lost in a human tidal wave, Rudel and Gregor gaze fixedly at the official platform where Perón, Brylcreemed and smug, is standing with his arms crossed. There is a sudden uproar as Evita appears. She blows kisses to her faithful, who kneel and wail, while confetti showers down from the balconies all around and, as in a stadium, torches, flags, fluttering handkerchiefs and bursting firecrackers greet the idol.

When the secretary-general of the CGT asks the crowd to proclaim her candidacy as vice president, Evita snuggles into El Líder's arms, stammers, asks for four days of reflection. Consternation all round. The crowd growls. Evita pleads, 'One day?' The crowd stamps. Evita begs, 'A few hours then?' No way. The choir chants her name for eighteen minutes, accompanied by '*Ahora, ahora*, now!' Evita sways, bursts into tears and declares that she will announce her decision that very evening on the radio.

Rudel and Gregor leave; they have had enough of her antics. They are deafened by the *bombos*, bass drums, and are disgusted by the *negrada*, the scum of the suburbs of Buenos Aires, all around them. Such a zoo would have been inconceivable in the Führer's Germany. To the two Nazis, the rally is symptomatic of Perón's comic-opera dictatorship. They see the Argentines as 'kings of psychodrama who obey orders without carrying them out. He who cannot obey will never be able to command'.

Away from the masses, Rudel entrusts an ultra-confidential rumour to Gregor: Evita is ill, very ill in fact. 'If it's true, our friend is screwed.'

Justicialism does not keep its promises. Pavements in central Buenos Aires are full of potholes; trains do not arrive on time; Perón spends compulsively and keeps very busy doing nothing; in Patagonia Richter has pulled a fast one, swallowing hundreds of millions of pesos without producing one watt of nuclear electricity; the Argentinian economy is on its knees and produces nothing of value. Rudel and Gregor see the harmful influence of Christianity. Perón fails to act with brutality because he is mired in all that Judaeo-Christian nonsense such as compassion and pity – all those forms of sentimentalism – which Nazism had eliminated.

Gregor despises the Catholic-fascist coterie surrounding El Líder. Weak men; all tigers without teeth, like Daye, a braggart who claims to have had tea with Hitler and the Shah of Iran. Perón's populist movement of international unity is pure hot air. His Third World War is a childish fantasy. Daye sinks into depression as he writes his memoirs; Mussolini's son launches himself in the textile industry; and Sabiani, former mayor of Marseille, drowns his loneliness in alcohol. When Marshal Pétain's death was announced a few weeks ago, they all gathered for a funereal vigil in Buenos Aires cathedral.

All these men are has-beens. They look to the past, while the Nazis of Buenos Aires scan the future: Germany.

20.

Their aim is to reconquer the Fatherland. The Dürer men's club does not believe in the 'democracy' imposed by the Allies. Their beloved Germany will not have changed with just a wave of a magic wand. They follow the news and comment in *Der Weg*. Its circulation continues to increase despite censorship and bans. They know that their fellow countrymen are nostalgic for the Wilhelmine Empire and the first years of the Third Reich, and that what is said about the 'atrocities' perpetrated in the camps is not believed. They howled for revenge after the Nuremberg trials. The Dürer men's club is convinced that the Germans have not disavowed Nazism. After all, the people voted for the regime and its conquests and revered the Führer. Gregor tells all to Sassen, Rudel and Fritsch: the enthusiasm of university academics and doctors in the 1930s; the jubilation that greeted the purge of all the old humanists and their radical reform programmes; the popularity of social Darwinism and racial hygiene throughout society; how prisoners in the camps were exploited by the giants of industry, becoming human guinea pigs in pharmaceutical laboratories; and how the gold fillings were stripped from the teeth of the Jews and sent to the Reichsbank every month.

The system profited everyone, until the chaos of the war's final years. Nobody protested when Jews were forced to kneel and clean the pavements. Nobody said a word when they disappeared overnight. If the world had not conspired against Germany, the Nazis would still be in power.

The Dürer men's club believes that Nazism will make a comeback. The men despise the trivial realities of their reinvented bourgeois life on the other side of the world, and are not content to run their businesses and fuck their mistresses. Germany's defeat merely interrupted a dazzling ascent. Thirty-year-old Fritsch, Sassen and Rudel fight on. They must act, and fast: the homeland is in danger. Adenauer is selling West Germany to the United States and making it part of western Europe, while East Germany is being plundered by the Soviets.

Yet they are hesitant. Assessing the strength of the movement back home is not so easy to arrange or carry out from so far away in Argentina. Should they form a government in exile? Foment revolution in Germany? Get rid of Adenauer by means of a coup d'état? The conspirators decide to follow Hitler's lead from twenty years before: enter the political fray, forge alliances, get into power through the ballot box. The next federal elections will be held in September 1953. Rudel is chosen by his comrades: the Germans have not forgotten his exploits.

In summer 1952, the air ace flies overseas to form a partnership with the Nazi militants of the Socialist Party of the Reich. The situation seems favourable to the designs of the Dürer men's club, following a scandal in Germany in September. Under the terms of the Luxembourg agreements, 'Rabbi Adenauer' (as Rudel calls him) recognises the guilt of the Germans and commits the German Federal Republic to pay billions of dollars in restitution to Israel and compensation to Jews. A month later, the chancellor succeeds in banning the Socialist Reich Party: Rudel returns to Buenos Aires and consults his co-conspirators. He then heads back to Germany, where he wins the support of the conservative nationalist Imperial Party. But, disconnected from the burgeoning economic growth back home, the Dürer men's club has made a mistake. Germans would rather holiday in Italy than pine for the lost days of Nazism. The same opportunism that incited them to serve the Reich now pushes them to embrace democracy. The German people bend with the wind, and the Imperial Party is wiped out in the 1953 federal elections.

21.

Gregor is eating a praline when he hears about his buddy Rudel's setbacks. He is lying on a brown leather sofa in the spacious sitting room of his apartment, which he moved into a few months ago, on the second floor of 431 Tacuari Street, in the centre of Buenos Aires. He has dispensed advice to Dürer's circle of friends, but has been content to follow their machinations from afar. He has never been a political animal. From his childhood on, irrespective of his professed love of Germany and his devotion to Nazism, he has always put himself first, and loved only himself. For wily Gregor, the end of 1953 is not only splendid, it is getting better by the day. No matter if Argentina is still in mourning and shrouded in misery for Evita, who has died of uterine cancer. No matter if Adenauer has thwarted the business affairs of Gregor's companions in exile. What does matter is secured. He has earned the respect of his peers and his business activities are flourishing. Gregor is having fun and getting rich.

He runs a carpentry works and a furniture factory financed by the inexhaustible supply of family money, practises illegal abortions and sells the famously tough Mengele agricultural machinery to farmers in Chaco and Santa Fe provinces. The family invests in South America, and one by one they make their way to Buenos Aires: his brother Alois visits with his wife; the faithful Sedlmeier comes several times; and the ageing but still formidable patriarch Karl Sr is expected soon. Mengele's father became a national socialist when it was expedient, in May 1933, and now – after running as an independent – he is the deputy mayor of Günzburg. Gregor worries about Karl Sr's imminent arrival. His father has always reproached him for marrying that 'little slut' Irene, and for not playing his part in the thriving business that Karl Mengele built from nothing. By the time he visits his eldest son, Karl has over six hundred employees.

At Gregor's place, Karl Sr admires the Dürer engraving and strokes the dog, Heinrich Lyons, 'a well-trained beast', and that's it. No warmth, no affection. True to himself, the captain of industry devotes all his energy to his business – in Buenos Aires as in Günzburg. Gregor serves as interpreter when Karl has meetings with Argentine businessmen, without mentioning that he is Karl's son, and introduces his father to his high-ranking friends. He is proud to be able to show off Klingenfuss, former diplomat of the Foreign Ministry's Jewish desk and now a bigwig in the German-Argentine Chamber of Commerce, and von Neurath, who has just become director of the Argentinian subsidiary of Siemens. A partnership is forged with Orbis, a promising company which manufactures stoves and ovens, run by Roberto Mertig, a Nazi from Dresden. The patriarch Mengele is seduced by Mertig's success and patriotism – all his employees are German. When they take leave of each other, father and son promise to meet up soon, in Europe perhaps.

Paraguay is the other Mengele hunting ground. As his father observed, Gregor is spending more and more time there with Rudel, who recovered from his electoral defeat by climbing Llullaillaco volcano, and frequenting Haase, whose wife is the daughter of the man who became finance minister after Paraguay's President Stroessner seized power in the May 1954 coup. Accompanied by Heinrich Lyons and his catalogues of agricultural equipment, Gregor criss-crosses the lush island of greenery that is surrounded by scrubland, palm savannah and the treeless wasteland of Gran Chaco, drawn there by the fields of maté and cotton. He visits cattle farmers, Mennonite communities and the descendants of the fanatical founders of Nueva Germania. He has developed valuable relationships across the entire country. Haase introduces him to Werner Jung, a former leader of Paraguay's Nazi youth group, and thanks to Rudel, Gregor also befriends Alejandro von Eckstein, the exiled Baltic baron who is captain of Stroessner's army and the dictator's brother-in-arms. They defeated the Bolivians together in the 1930s in an absurd desert war, absurd because despite the claims of the general staff, there was not a drop of oil in the Chaco.

Gregor tells himself that Paraguay would be a good hide-away if Argentina fell apart. An assassination attempt almost cost Perón his life in April 1953; the economic situation is deteriorating; inflation is skyrocketing; steelworkers are on strike; and wages are falling. El Líder presses the levers of economic policy according to his capricious whims and moods like a child at the controls of an aeroplane. Since the death of Evita, whose body he has had embalmed, Perón has been disorientated. He gorges on ravioli in his residence at Olivos, and regularly hosts very young girls, whom he teaches to ride mopeds. Nelly, his new companion, is thirteen years old; when she is a good girl, he allows her to wear Evita's jewels. The press claims he has had a fling with the actress Gina Lollobrigida; the Church is upset by the presidential orgies. Everybody refers to him by the nickname El Pocho, the spoiled one.

Gregor has seen it for himself: Perón has ugly bags under his eyes. Sassen and Rudel ended up keeping their promise to engineer an introduction. During their brief meeting, the president played absent-mindedly with his poodles while the three Nazis looked on admiringly. He exchanged only a few words with Gregor. His grandfather was a doctor, he said, and he, too, would have liked to study medicine, but to the delight of the Argentines, the hand of God had guided him to military school.

Perón then dismissed the men with a sweeping gesture as his new favourite was announced: Brother Tommy Hicks, an American healer.

22.

Gregor is always smartly dressed and entertaining and has a good reputation in the German community of Buenos Aires. Considered an intellectual, he punctuates his sentences with quotations from Goethe and the philosopher Johann Fichte. Women gush about his almost ceremonial courtesy and impressive knowledge of German culture. There is only one man on whom his charm has zero effect. Sassen introduced him one day, when Gregor was enjoying luncheon at the ABC in his usual place beneath the Bavarian coat of arms. As he greeted the balding, drab fellow, he knew immediately that they would not get along. Ricardo Klement's hand was moist; his sidelong gaze was shielded by thick-framed, crooked glasses.

Sassen could not stop himself from blurting out their true identity. 'Adolf Eichmann, meet Josef Mengele; Josef Mengele, meet Adolf Eichmann.' To Eichmann the name of Mengele means nothing. Captains, SS doctors . . . the great architect of the Holocaust has come across hundreds and thousands of them. Mengele was the overseer of lowly works, a mosquito in the eyes of Eichmann, who makes him feel like one during their initial encounter, while sedulously reminding the doctor of his, Eichmann's, dazzling ascent to the most esoteric levels of the Third Reich; the crushing weight of his responsibilities; his power. 'Everyone knew who I was! The richest Jews kissed my feet in a bid to save their lives.'

Eichmann also hid in a farm before emigrating to Argentina; he worked in northern Germany as a forester and also raised chickens. Then he was in Tucumán, leading a team of surveyors for Capri, the state-owned firm founded by Perón to employ Nazis and build hydroelectric plants. When Capri went bankrupt in 1953, Eichmann, his wife and their three boys settled in Chacabuco Street, Buenos Aires, in the Olivos neighbourhood.

Gregor actively tries to avoid the Klements, as they call themselves, but his move in early 1954 to the ground floor of beautiful Moorish house nearby – 1875 Sarmiento Street – means that he often bumps into them, especially the children, who are invariably dressed as gauchos, as though for Carnival. Eichmann is like a fairground attraction. He is invited to meetings on board the *Falken* and country house parties at Menge's place. Nazi society seems bewitched by his evil aura. When Sassen talks about him, you would think he had gained access to Himmler, Goering and Heydrich all in one, since Eichmann boasts that he was close to them. Wherever he goes, in Nazi circles, Eichmann gets drunk, plays the violin, creates a drama. He presents himself as the Great Inquisitor and the Czar of the Jews. The Grand Mufti of Jerusalem was a friend. He had an official chauffeur-driven car so he could terrorise Europe as he pleased. Ministers ran after him and stepped aside to let him pass. He enjoyed the most beautiful women from Budapest. Sometimes, at the end of an evening, he will autograph photos for his admirers: 'Adolf Eichmann, SS-Obersturmbannführer retired'.

Eichmann's quest for notoriety irritates Gregor, who has been so very careful ever since he landed. He has only revealed his true identity and the nature of his activities in Auschwitz to a few very close friends. He sketches out to everyone else a vague career outline: military doctor, German, in the New World to start a new life. When he bumps into Eichmann, a former tradesman, an uneducated accountant's son who never finished secondary school and never experienced battle at the front, he despises him. Eichmann is a pathetic creature, a failure of the highest order; even the laundry business that he opened in Olivos has already closed down. He is also a bitter man who resents Gregor's attractive house, his bachelor's life and new car – a superb German Borgward Isabella coupe. The dislike is mutual. As far as Eichmann is concerned, Mengele, whatever name he is using these days, is a dark-skinned, yellow-bellied daddy's boy: the scum of the earth.

23.

Gregor takes the picture out of the frame and burns it at the window; soon all that remains of the portrait is a small cluster of ashes. A sudden draft scatters them in the warm Buenos

Aires air. Irene is filing for a divorce in order to marry the shoe salesman from Freiburg. Gregor calls Haase and Rudel; he needs a good Argentine defence attorney to get in touch with her lawyer in Günzburg. Money is not a problem, but he wants to have lots of intermediaries between them, like screens, and he refuses to do his former wife any favours. The divorce is finalised, in Düsseldorf, on 25 March 1954.

'Excellent news,' Karl Sr writes succinctly. 'At last you've got rid of the bitch. You must stop dreaming of winning her back; at your age, it's indecent.' Patriarch Mengele is particularly pleased with the divorce because he has a Machiavellian plan in mind. A three-way hit involving his precious company, Josef, and another problematic bitch: Martha, Karl Jr's widow, who is destined to inherit her deceased husband's shares in the family business. For a while now, Martha has been in love. Karl Sr is afraid that if she marries the foreigner who is the object of her affections, he will sit on the board of directors. Karl suggests to Josef that he marry his sister-in-law so that the company will stay in the hands of the Mengele family. He can then give all his shares to Martha after their marriage: that way, in the event of an arrest warrant being issued against him, the company will not be paralysed. Whatever happens, Josef will dictate to Martha her decisions on the board of directors.

Lying in a deck chair in the garden of the Moorish house, Gregor blesses his father's genius and gloats over the idea of hitching up with the widow of his hated brother, anticipating Irene's dismay and anger when she finds out that he, too, has remarried, and with Martha to boot: Martha whom she loathes.

Karl Sr advises Josef to meet his sister-in-law in the Swiss Alps. 'You will travel under your false identity using an Argentinian passport. You know enough people in Buenos Aires to get hold of one easily. I'll bring Martha back to her senses and take care of everything else . . . tickets, accommodation, transfers. And I'll arrange for Rolf to accompany her. It's high time you meet your son.'

24.

Gregor begins the administrative process in spring 1955. Despite his ability to call on his relatives and bundles of dollars, it will be as long-drawn-out as the Perónist bureaucracy is labyrinthine. And Gregor has only a residence permit, so he must create a substantial file (recommendations, guarantees, certificates of good conduct, corresponding certificates) before he can apply for a noncitizen's national passport. He waits almost a year, and in the meantime Argentina descends into violence and counter-revolution.

On 16 June 1955, the 'Gorillas', anti-Perónist military leaders, bomb the presidential palace and May Square. Perón escapes the coup but his days as leader of Argentina are numbered. The Church, refuge of all opposition, wants him dead for the way that he has cancelled subsidies to religious schools, legalised divorce and prostitution, and encouraged the proliferation of sects under the influence of Brother Tommy. 'Yes to Perón! No to priests!': there are demonstrations and counter-demonstrations, Perón the Antichrist throws priests in prison, the Church excommunicates him, chapels are ransacked and the austral winter of anarchy has begun. For every Perónist killed, El Pocho swears to kill five of his enemies. By September, when Gregor finally completes all the necessary paperwork, rumours of a coup d'état are rife; mutinies flare up in Córdoba and the port of Bahía Blanca. On 16 September, the navy blockades Buenos Aires and threatens to bomb the refineries. The rebels greet one another with the words 'God is just'.

Argentina is on the verge of civil war, and Perón resigns. He burns his most compromising files, and to avoid being hanged from a lamppost like his mentor Mussolini, he escapes on a Paraguayan gunboat bound for Asunción. A military junta led by an alcoholic general takes power. A few weeks later, the general is deposed by another general, the remorseless Pedro Eugenio Aramburu, who promises to purge Argentina of Perónism.

Sitting in front of his radio cabinet, Gregor listens to the martial tones of Aramburu hammering out his orders: 'Anyone who exhibits images or sculptures of the fugitive tyrant and his deceased spouse, or who utters in public words or phrases such as Perón, Perónism, "third way" and vaunts the merits of the fallen dictatorship will be punished by a prison sentence from six months to three years.' In the name of the Liberating Revolution, union leaders are arrested, thousands of officials dismissed. All places named Perón (cities, neighbourhoods, provinces, streets, stations, squares, pools, racetracks, stadiums, dance halls) are renamed; little Evitas change their first name. Her foundation is closed, her sheets are burned, her cutlery is melted down; the statues are toppled; and the mopeds and ornaments owned by the fallen couple are exhibited to make a show of their vice and greed. Evita's embalmed corpse disappears. Borges is appointed head of the National Library and professor at the Buenos Aires Faculty of Letters. Perón takes refuge in Panama; it is a gilded exile involving cabarets, cigarettes, whiskey and gorgeous call-girls, and he falls for a dancer, María Estela Martínez, soon to be his third wife, whom he renames Isabel.

The Nazis are uneasy now that their protector has flown. Aramburu has promised to break the bones of the profiteers of the previous regime. Several companies backed by German capital have to close down. Police search the home of Rudel in Córdoba and put him under house arrest. Bohne and other war criminals leave Argentina. Daye notes in his diary that 'the fruits of exile are bitter'. Gregor thinks of escaping to Paraguay but changes his mind: he has steered clear of politics and was never part of Perón's inner circle. He is just an honest entrepreneur. He stops performing illegal abortions and waits for the storm to pass. Aramburu admires Prussian military traditions, so maybe he'll get along with the Nazis.

Gregor ends up getting a three-month passport. On 22 March 1956, he boards a Pan Am DC-7 and lands in Geneva after a short stopover in New York.

25.

Sedlmeier is waiting for him at the airport and drives him to Engelberg, the ski resort, and to Hotel Engel, the town's grandest four-star hotel.

He is greeted at the reception desk by two twelve-year-old boys accompanied by an attractive brunette: Martha, her son Karl-Heinz and his own son, Rolf.

26.

Martha hums in front of the bathroom mirror as the water fills the bath. Lying on the bed in the adjoining room where a fire crackles in the hearth, hands behind his head, Gregor listens to the happy woman and the lapping sounds. He looks out of the window at the falling snow and smiles with pleasure. His Swiss sojourn is proving to be idyllic, and the pure mountain air is invigorating. Martha introduced him to the children as Uncle Fritz from America. Rolf had been told when he was little that his father Josef had died in combat in Russia, just after he was born.

Rolf and Karl-Heinz are punctual, disciplined boys. They sit up straight at table and only speak when Mengele-Gregor-Fritz authorises them to do so. They look up to him: Uncle Fritz is a world-class skier, having served with the Alpine troops, and they love his stories. At dinner, out walking, in the evenings, they urge him to tell all. Karl-Heinz wants to hear stories about tank battles, heroism and camaraderie on the dusty steppes of Russia; Rolf's imagination is captured by the Andean epic of San Martín and the adventures of gauchos and pampas Indians, 'on the banks of the muddy River Plate, which snakes toward the blue whales of the ocean'. Uncle Fritz describes the conquest of the Argentinian desert, of the 'triumph of civilization over savage barbarism which is similar to that of Germans in the eastern territories during the war. Never forget, children, the Germans were more talented than the Greeks and stronger than the Romans.'

Gregor observes his son whenever he gets the chance. Rolf has his mother's hands and nose, her veiled melancholic eyes, her fragile beauty and artlessness. He is less self-assured than Karl-Heinz, who is taller than he is by a head and skis a lot better. Karl-Heinz is on his way to being a man, while Rolf is still a child. Fireman, astronaut, engineer: he has no idea what he will do later, and changes his mind every day. Gregor was more resolute at his age.

His inner spark is revived and he fans it, remembering the boy he once was. He was obsessed with the microscope that his father had given to him on his tenth birthday. He was convinced that he would be as famous one day as his idols of yesteryear:

Dr Robert Koch, the founding father of modern bacteriology, and August Kekulé, who discovered the structure of benzene and that carbon is tetravalent. He realised early on that the high priests, the stars, of the twentieth century would be doctors and researchers. He recalled how Serge Voronoff had made headline news when he transplanted the testicles of young chimpanzees on to wealthy elderly patients in his clinic on the Côte d'Azur; the press had made hay of his exploits in the 1920s. Voronoff may have been a charlatan, but Germany was well and truly a paradise for modern medicine; for science. Biology, zoology, aspirin, the microscope and laboratories were all German inventions. He had already decided at the age of fifteen that he would not sit and rot in Günzburg, in thrall to his father. But from Karl Sr he inherited tenacity, malice and ambition, and from Walburga, his mother, a clinical coldness and a shrivelled heart.

Gregor sees in his mind's eye the student he was in Munich, Vienna and Frankfurt. The 1930s were a time of great upheaval; an exhilarating era. While his classmates sparred, drank and played at being big shots in the S.A., he worked hard, and his industry duly paid off. He was spotted by the highest-placed dignitaries: Eugen Fischer, the illustrious eugenicist who witnessed the Herero and Namaqua Genocide in Namibia at the beginning of the twentieth century, and Prof. Mollinson, an expert on heredity and racial hygiene and supervisor of his thesis ('Racial-Morphological Examination of the Anterior Portion of the Lower Jaw in Four Racial Groups', awarded *summa cum laude*). Mollinson recommended him to the most famous German geneticist, Baron Otmar von Verschuer, a specialist in twins. Gregor became his research assistant at just twenty-six and was soon a favourite at the University of Frankfurt's Institute for Hereditary Biology and Racial Hygiene. When Freiherr von Verschuer became the director of the Kaiser Wilhelm Institute for Anthropology, Human Heredity and Eugenics in Berlin, he sent Mengele to Auschwitz with the words: 'The largest laboratory in history, a badge of honour for a brilliant and diligent young researcher. You may well discover the secrets of multiple births.' The baron financed his research and Mengele regularly sent him samples – marrow, eyes, blood, organs, skeletons – and the results of his experiments. He was not idle during his twenty-one months at the camp. He scoured the selection ramp with unparalleled rigor, deinfested hundreds of barracks and prevented several epidemics of typhus. His zeal was rewarded once again, this time with an Iron Cross – second degree with swords – along with appreciative eulogies from his superiors.

'Rolf needs to be taken in hand,' Gregor says to himself in the large, balconied, four-star hotel suite. 'He will never toughen up at the hands of his mother and the shoe merchant from Freiburg.' He is convinced that women don't like wimps. They like virile, determined men like him. Martha sensed it immediately: he is made of tougher stuff than his dead brother.

During their first evening together, as the boys eat their supper, Uncle Fritz undresses her with his eyes. His gaze lingers over her black hair tied up in a bun, her red lips, her horsey mouth. When she gets up to go to the lavatory, her fleshy rounded rump triggers his desire – the undulating gait of Martha Mengele, née Weil, was a legend in Günzburg. She may not have Irene's distinction nor her ethereal quality, but here and now in the Hotel Engel, Gregor vows to think no more of his ex-wife, and never to compare the two women again. Martha has character and sound beliefs; Rolf and Karl-Heinz obey her; she is a committed Nazi, a caring mother, and – despite not being beautiful – she is a sensual woman in her mid-thirties. Most importantly, she is his younger brother Karl's widow. When Gregor took off her lacy bra on their second night together, he had the marvellous feeling of giving the final coup de grace to his brother, of burying him for a second time.

'If only he could see me take his woman,' he leers to himself, jumping off the bed.

He undresses and goes into the bathroom. Martha is waiting for him in the bath.

27.

Sedlmeier's Mercedes purrs in front of the hotel. Martha and the boys will return home by train, Gregor by car with his friend. He has not been in Günzburg since November 1944.

As they cross over snow-covered passes, Gregor tenses up. Luncheon on the banks of Lake Constance changes nothing.

His pulse quickens, and when after nightfall he recognises the loop of the Danube at the city's entrance, the Renaissance castle and the Baroque church, he asks Sedlmeier to be quiet, because he is feeling so anxious.

So here he is, in the big grey house of his childhood. Apart from a painting in the entrance hall and the urns containing his mother and his brother on a mantelpiece, nothing has changed. Gregor rediscovers the dark wood panelling, the Biedermeier console, the gramophone in the dining room where he eats with Sedlmeier, his brother and his father, who has given time off to the governess and the cook at his insistence. Gregor thanks them for it. The hotel was sublime, the boys in glowing health and Martha gorgeous. The plan has worked, he will marry her, willingly, but a cloud of gloom descends: he should not have come to Günzburg. What will he do here? Missing since the end of the war, Josef Mengele is hardly going to strut down Augsburger Strasse! Or in front of the factory, for that matter. Everyone will recognise him, people will gossip, and the city is not a big place: to take such a risk would be insane.

Karl Sr tries to reassure him. Günzburg is his fiefdom; the family firm is a small empire and by far the largest employer in the city, and no one would dare to denounce the boss's son – and to whom, anyhow? He is not a wanted man in Germany; an arrest warrant has not been issued. 'Enough is enough, Josef, you're always so timorous. This is your home, for goodness' sake! People remember you well and often talk about your brilliant studies. Adenauer's chief of staff, Mr Globke, doesn't worry about the past as he goes into his office in the Chancellery every morning. Everyone knows that he annotated the Nuremberg laws and ordained that Jews with non-Jewish names take on the additional first names of Israël and Sara. So what? Nobody cares, certainly not Adenauer. Just like nobody cares where you were during the war! You did your duty, and that's that.' Alois tries to soothe Karl Sr, who seems less forceful these last months. He tells Josef that their father has never been so powerful and adored by his employees; he will even be an honorary citizen soon. 'Günzburg would fall apart without us. We are financing new social housing, a hospital and a swimming pool. Father will distribute sausages to all the children to celebrate his seventy-fifth birthday.'

Gregor cannot sleep. Ten days of winter sports have softened him, weakened his defences, thrown him to the wolves – he has premonitions. Even if he stays indoors all week, the worst could happen at any moment. His name is on a list of war criminals, no one can be trusted, his family understands nothing. The next day, he decides, he will pay a visit to an friend from the SS Panzer Division Wiking, a pharmacist in Munich, with whom he hid for a month before going to the farm, after recovering his notes and samples in the Soviet Zone at the start of his escape. The anonymity of the big city is better. He will go by car; Sedlmeier can rent an Opel in Gregor's name. And assuming all goes well, he can still spend a few days in Günzburg. He has to talk business with the family: Argentina, Paraguay and maybe Chile.

Gregor curses as he listens to the news on the car radio. The Bundeswehr will take part in NATO manoeuvres, a priest is praised for creating a Judaeo-Christian circle of friendship in Frankfurt, the Israeli Trade Mission in Cologne welcomes a new director. And bloody jazz: Gregor tries to find a station that broadcasts classical music. He glances down, fiddles with the buttons for a second or two, and crashes into a car that has braked suddenly in front of him.

Gregor is accommodating to the driver and offers cash. The bumper is barely scratched, what's the point of writing a report? It's raining, let's not waste time. The lady is swathed in a fur coat. She refuses, saying the law is the law. 'This is Germany, a civilised country.' Her husband's silver BMW has just come out of the garage. Gregor insists on simply paying for the damage, adding thirty marks to his offer. She gets a bundle of documents from the glove box; he gets aggressive, threatens to leave, she calls the police; rubberneckers gather, a man in an overcoat makes a note of the Opel's number plate, and a patrol car suddenly appears. Puzzled by his Argentine papers and his heavy Bavarian accent, the officer orders Gregor not to leave Munich until his identity has been verified.

When the police finally go away, Gregor runs to a phone booth. He is trembling as he dials his father's number. Two hours later, an imposing delegation heads for police head-quarters in central Munich. Karl Sr, his lawyer, the chief of police of Günzburg and Sedlmeier, black briefcase in hand. They find the reporting officer, go out for a beer, parley, haggle and tie up a deal.

Gregor flies to South America the next day.

28.

His life is in Argentina and Martha and Karl-Heinz will join him there. At forty-five, Gregor wants peace and a new home: a big house in which to welcome them. He spots a California-style villa at 970 Virrey Vertiz, an unassuming and wooded street in a residential part of Olivos, close by the shoreline. Martha and Karl-Heinz will not be disorientated. The place is superb and is reminiscent of the Alster Lakes in Hamburg and the Wannsee in Berlin.

Despite his fortune, Gregor has to borrow money to buy his house and carry out the mission entrusted to him by his father: to invest in a pharmaceutical company, Fadro Farm. Mertig, the director of Orbis, his South American partner, advised him to do so, and some of his friends have started making medicines and researching specialised treatments for tuberculosis. The banks will not lend a peso to a stateless person whose passport is about to expire. If he wants to settle down and remarry, Gregor has to retrieve his identity and become Mengele once more.

Gregor consults his circle of friends, as usual. He is not risking anything in Argentina. The Americans have just one priority, fighting the Soviets, and the Germans do not want to hear about Nazism. The war is over. Schwammberger, who exterminated thousands of Jews in Poland, got a passport; the

German consulate did not make trouble. And the new ambassador is a splendid fellow, Sassen tells him. Werner Junker was a Nazi and a close collaborator of Ribbentrop's at the Ministry of Foreign Affairs. He was stationed in the Balkans and is delighted to find his old friend Pavelić, the former Croatian dictator, in Buenos Aires.

Gregor goes to the embassy, where he provides all the information he has been trying to conceal since the end of the war to prove that he is Josef Mengele. The consular officer does not blink when Gregor declares he has lived under a false identity since arriving in Argentina. He sends the file to Bonn, where no one checks the lists of wanted war criminals. Gregor may have panicked for nothing in Munich: the German Federal Republic condemns Nazism but reintegrates its executives and henchmen, compensates the Jews yet lets their killers go about their business in South America and the Middle East. Recognition of the right to 'political error', an amnesty for the 'victims of denazification', national cohesion, generalised amnesia . . . farewell Gregor. In September 1956, the West German Consulate in Buenos Aires issues a civil registration form and a birth certificate to Josef Mengele.

He has to regularise his status with the Argentine authorities. He goes to court and is fingerprinted by the police. No magistrate is offended by his lies; he is neither pursued nor punished; a great many Germans have had a memory bypass. *Benvenido, Señor Mengele*: he is given a new residence permit in November, number 3,940,484. Back at the consulate, he receives a German passport in his name: Josef Mengele;

DOB 16 March 1911, in Günzburg; address 1875 Sarmiento Street, Buenos Aires; height 1.74m; eyes green-brown; entrepreneur and cabinet-maker of wooden furniture and toys. In the photograph he has provided, a moustache adorns his olive-skinned face.

Martha and Karl-Heinz arrive in Buenos Aires. Mengele gets the loan and buys the splendid, coveted house. Adjoining Perón's former private residence, it boasts a garden and a swimming pool. Martha is registered in the directory and his nephew Karl-Heinz is introduced as his son.

The pasha knows all the right people and is becoming a respectable *bourgeois*.

Fortune is smiling on him.

29.

In November 1956, Fritz Bauer, prosecutor general of the state of Hesse, issues an arrest warrant for Adolf Eichmann, 'wherever he is'. A homosexual Jewish social democrat, Bauer was excluded from the civil service and interned in a concentration camp by the Gestapo before fleeing to Scandinavia. Since returning to Germany in the late 1940s, Bauer has made it his mission to force his compatriots to face their past.

30.

The world gradually finds out about the extermination of European Jews. More and more books, articles, documentaries are devoted to the concentration camps and the Nazi annih–ilation programme. In 1956, *Night and Fog*, directed by Alain Resnais, has a profound and traumatic impact, despite the efforts of the West German government, which manages to get the film removed from the official selection of the Cannes Film Festival in the name of Franco-German reconciliation. *The Diary of Anne Frank* grows in popularity. There is talk of crimes against humanity, the Final Solution, and 6 million murdered Jews.

The Dürer men's club denies this statistic. It celebrates the extermination programme while putting estimates at just 365,000 Jewish victims. Mass murder, loaded trucks and poison-gas chambers are vehemently denied. The figure of 6 million Jewish deaths is fake history, yet another Zionist conspiracy, created with the aim of making Germany feel guilty for declar-ing war and bringing upon itself destruction culminating in 7 million dead, its most beautiful cities razed to the ground, its ancestral lands in the east lost. For Sassen and Fritsch, only one man is capable of reinstating the truth: Adolf Eichmann. He oversaw every stage of the meticulously planned war against the Jews. Since the death of Hitler, Himmler and Heydrich, he is the ultimate expert, the last key witness. He knows the chief protagonists and the numbers; he can disown and deny. The Jews have dragged Germany into the mud; Eichmann will restore its honour. They devised the biggest lie in history to seize British-controlled Palestine and will be publicly denounced. Their masks and those of their supporters will slip: the Dürer men's club will undermine their plotting and work for the rehabilitation of Germany, for the redemption of Nazism and the Führer.

Fritsch and Sassen suggest to Eichmann that he expound his thoughts on 'the pseudo–final solution' in the form of a book, to be released by Dürer Publishing. Eichmann is delighted by the idea. Since his laundry closed down, he has worked in a company which makes bathroom appliances, and for lack of anything better farms Angora rabbits and hens under the harsh sun of the pampas. His days are long and monotonous. He feeds the animals, cleans up their cages and their shit, ruminates over the glories of yesteryear. His family has stayed in Buenos Aires, where his fourth son, Ricardo Francisco, has just been born – a miracle, as his wife is forty-six years old and he is fifty. He earns a modest living. So a book about his Master Plan would mean the end of anonymity and chicken farming; it is a godsend. He will be a star reborn and be able to defend his reputation. As a zealous reader of newspapers and history books, he is well aware that his name regularly crops up, often inaccurately, and this offends him. His children must know the truth. The German people will rise to support him, and his family

71

will be able to return to Europe with their heads held high. And in the meantime Eichmann, Fritsch and Sassen will earn a great deal of money from book sales.

31.

The recording sessions start in April 1957 in the Dutch journalist's opulent home. Every Sunday men and women gather around the man who masterminded the Holocaust. He is flattered by all the attention and is delighted to savour the cigars and malt whiskey supplied by his host. Eichmann plays with his SS Honour ring as he answers the questions of Sassen and Fritsch, sometimes assisted by guests with sharper skills: the great Bubi von Alvensleben, Himmler's higher SS and police leader, and Dieter Menge, the fanatical veteran pilot who owns the sprawling cattle ranch where the Nazis like to meet.

Despite Sassen's insistence, Mengele refuses to join the sessions. He has no intention of listening to the boasts of an embittered fool, and duly warns his friend: Eichmann will get them into trouble, his name is in the press, the German judiciary is after him, and sooner or later, if he does not shut his big mouth, the real man behind the pseudonym 'Klement' will be exposed. Mengele does not want any publicity. He has better things to do. Namely, get rich and screw Martha.

He returns from a one-week holiday in Chile. Rudel's small private plane landed in Santiago, where an old friend of the pilot's was waiting for them: Walter Rauff, the 'Butcher of Milan' (97,000 murders), inventor of the Black Raven gas van which was the model for the gas chambers in the extermination camps. The three men explored the desert volcanoes of Atacama, swam naked in turquoise lagoons and camped under limpid and starry skies.

Back in Argentina, Mengele, Martha and Karl-Heinz, accompanied by their loyal pooch, enjoy weekends away, by the ocean in Mar del Plata and in Tigre, the city strewn with canals and islands covered with trees in bloom, on the delta of the Paraná River and the Río de la Plata. They stay at the Tigre Hotel, which has been visited by the Prince of Wales and legendary tenor Caruso. Since Martha's arrival in Argentina, Mengele has rediscovered the splendours of Buenos Aires with her on his arm. They admire the German fountain on Libertador Avenue, the English clock tower in front of the Retiro railway station, and the Art Deco style of the Kavanagh Building in San Martín Square. The couple go to the theatre and to concerts, dine with the Haases and Mertigs, take Karl-Heinz to the San Isidro Racecourse. They go shopping among the elegant and parvenu clientele of the department store Gath & Chaves.

It is 1957 and life is sweet. Mengele savours the charms of the newly instituted routine: supervising Karl-Heinz's homework, relishing Martha's thighs and cuisine; polishing the chrome of his toy, the Borgward Isabella coupe, and excursions to the brothel with wicked Sassen, though less often than before.

The future looks bright, the worst is behind him, and Mengele feels safe. He has sold his furniture factory to put capital into Fadro Farm. He plunges with gleeful delight into medical and scientific journals and works on his old notes, completing them. He has not given up on landing a position as a university professor, continuing his work on human genetic improvement and achieving glory.

Meanwhile, Sassen and Fritsch continue to interview Eichmann. For six months he delivers, with pride, a monologue expressing 'the indefatigable spirit of the abiding German'. At times he is moved to tears by his experiences and his achievements – '6 million Jews eliminated' – as well as his regret that he did not accomplish his mission, 'the total annihilation of the enemy'. Eichmann confirms the full extent of the extermination programme to Sassen, Fritsch and the Dürer men's club, who did not want to believe in 'enemy propaganda'. He details the mass killings, the gas chambers and the ovens, the forced labour, the death marches and the famines: the total war ordered by the Führer.

Sassen and Fritsch, such lambs to the slaughter, believed that Nazism was pure. They were not expecting Eichmann's razor-sharp verification. Or rather, they hoped that Hitler had been betrayed and that Eichmann had been manipulated by foreign powers. They are disturbed by the figure of 6 million. Once the interviews are finished, they put some distance between themselves and this perpetrator of crimes against humanity. They have played their trump card and lost. Sassen keeps the precious tapes, but Dürer Publishing cancels the book. Yugoslav secret agents shoot at Pavelić, who flees to Uruguay. Adenauer wins the elections again in autumn 1957. The Central Office for the Investigation of National Socialist Crimes is established the following year, in Ludwigsburg. Nazism has no future in Germany: a page is definitively turned.

The magazine *Der Weg* founders; Fritsch closes his publishing house and moves to Austria early in 1958. Banned from publishing, he becomes a night porter at a big hotel in Salzburg.

With no fixed income following Fritsch's departure, Sassen dedicates himself to his journalistic career, using different pseudonyms, and dreams of returning to Europe. He, too, would like to benefit from the economic miracle. Eichmann is gloomy and frustrated but has not given up on being heard. He plans to go to court in Germany, convinced that his honour and reputation can be rehabilitated after a sensational trial in which he'll play the starring role. His sons and acquaintances dissuade him. He now has a low-ranking job in Mertig's company, Orbis, after his chicken and rabbit farm goes bankrupt.

Mengele is not surprised by these disasters. He despises these drawing-room Nazis: Eichmann the braggart, Sassen the sensitive pornographer and snotty-nosed Fritsch. He watched, he knew, and he acted without remorse or regret. Mengele avoids Sassen and flees from Eichmann, and he advises all the Nazis in Buenos Aires to follow suit: 'Eichmann is dangerous.'

Other exciting projects await.

32.

On 25 July 1958, Josef Mengele marries Martha Mengele in Nueva Helvecia, Uruguay. The wedding is unremarkable and very private. Karl-Heinz, Rudel and Sedlmeier are the witnesses, and Mertig and Haase and friends from Paraguay are guests, along with Jung, former head of the Hitler Youth – now a businessman – and von Eckstein, the Baltic baron. Sassen was not invited, and an ailing Karl Sr resigned himself to staying in Günzburg. Alois preferred to grace his box at the Bayreuth Festival. A reckless driver ran over Heinrich Lyons two weeks before the ceremony. As soon as toasts have been drunk and lunch eaten (smoked trout and saveloy salad; venison goulash; plum strudel; Riesling Moselle 1947), the Mengeles entrust their son to Haase, pack up their bags and leave: the road to Bariloche is a long one.

Martha curls up against Josef at the wheel of the Borgward Isabella. The wind whistles over the bonnet as the coupe skims along. The spinach-green pampas gives way to rocky terrain and vast skies flecked with purplish swallows and black eagles. Kilometre upon kilometre of thorny trails criss-cross the seemingly never-ending countryside. Then the road rises and jagged mountains rear up before them like rows of sharks' teeth: the craggy Andes, an Argentine Tyrol. The Mengeles skirt a celestial lake washed clear of snow to reach Bariloche and their palace, at last.

The Llao Llao Hotel is sublime. A bouquet of flowers and chocolates await the newlyweds in their deluxe, although soberly furnished, room. The breathtaking panoramic view from their terrace takes in Lake Nahuel Huapi and Lake Moreno, which circle the peninsula and the hilltop hotel. Llao Llao's grand buildings with sloping roofs are like a medieval German village protected from the villainy and chaos of the world. The spit-roasted Patagonian lamb they enjoy on their first evening is succulent. Martha is happy. As the mist evaporates at dawn, she trembles before such beauty: the titanic landscape with its purple peaks, the dazzling rays of light that pierce the forests of Antarctic beech and snowy oak. Josef, who had a restless night, is buried under the covers, still fast asleep.

He is disconcerted by their honeymoon. He would have never thought he could tolerate the presence of another woman. Martha is gentle and patient, receptive to his opinions about the fall of Rome and to his long monologues during their hikes when he recounts the tumultuous lives of Wagner and Albrecht von Haller, the founding father of German biology and the first to perform anatomical experiments on animal organs. Strangely, too, he has never before felt more desire than he has for this woman with big teeth and pudgy fingers. Martha is a fountain of youth, a lover who transports him down unknown avenues. When they get back to Buenos Aires he gives her a house by the ocean in a seaside resort.

After the war, a strong contingent of Nazis was welcomed in Bariloche, along with numerous Austrians, delighted to don skis again, and a Flemish painter, the former chief of Hitlerite propaganda in occupied Belgium. Kopps, the former chief of Himmler's spy service, whom Gregor met at the offices of *Der Weg*, has opened a hotel, the Campana, and the best grocer's shop in town, the Wien delicatessen, belongs to SS Capt. Erich Priebke, who was involved in the Ardeatine Caves massacre of 335 civilians in Rome. Rudel is a regular visitor who belongs to the city's Andean Club and gives members' contact details to Mengele.

They all meet up one evening over a fondue. Rauff has crossed the Chilean border to congratulate the youthful married couple. The Nazis talk about the good old days, for the umpteenth time, and reminisce about Richter, the atomic scientist who pulled a fast one on Perón, sinking the dictator's millions into his fake nuclear reactor and secret laboratory on Huemul island, just off Bariloche. Anecdotes abound, glasses tinkle, Kopps announces that a massive Judaeo-Masonic plot is being hatched at the White House and the Kremlin. Mengele yawns and embraces Martha. He prefers the thrilling sex he has with his wife to the society of these manly companions with their breath stinking of bad *eau-de-vie*.

The following day, Martha and Josef climb through clearings and woods. Their footsteps crunch on the snow, which falls in big flakes, and they stop for lunch on a promontory from which they have to imagine the valley below. Mengele is on the edge of the precipice when a hazy sun pierces the cottony mass and unveils the glacier-peaks, the blue lakes: enchanting nature. Suddenly dizzy, like a traveller contemplating a sea of clouds painted by Caspar David Friedrich, he opens his arms wide and roars with laughter. His chest expands, his blood thunders and his temples throb. Martha speaks to him but he does not hear her, absorbed as he is by his thoughts, so happy, so proud. In this verminous, ruined world deserted by God, he has freedom, money, success; no one has arrested him and no one ever will.

33.

A pile of mail is waiting for Mengele when the couple get back home. There is a letter from his father and a police summons among the invoices and advertising leaflets: he should have reported to Olivos police station three days earlier. Mengele is on the telephone talking to his lawyer when a neighbour rings at the door, insistently, looking tormented. The police came yesterday and the day before. The police are on the doorstep now. Mengele has not even unstrapped his luggage when two strong sergeants handcuff him and bundle him into their van, sirens screaming.

The previous day's papers are thrown into his face by a cop. In two conservative dailies he reads 'The Butchers of Buenos Aires', 'The Doctors of Death' and 'The murderer wears white shoes' on the front page of *Detective* magazine. The daughter of a great industrialist has died following an abortion; she was not even fifteen. It's scandalous! In custody, her doctor denounced his colleagues to the police, who have dismantled a whole network. In Argentina, there is great rejoicing as all these heads roll. 'The doctor gave us the name of a certain Gregor – you, Josef Mengele,' growls the cop. 'You're in a right old mess: illegal medical practice, clandestine abortions, corrupting the moral order of a nation generous enough to welcome you.' Mengele plays with his moustache, flatly denies the charges, his lawyer by his side, and has a rethink. 'It was a long time ago; I just tried to give a helping hand, a couple of successful operations . . . I strongly condemn my actions and have no intention of starting up again. Officer, why don't we come to arrangement and hush up this nasty business?'

The cop rubs his eyes but says nothing. Mengele is banged up. The superhero is in agony. The cell stinks of urine, the mattress is infested with lice, the broth given to him by his jailers, morning, noon and night, is foul. On the third day, the cop sends for him. 'OK. How much?' Mengele doubles, then triples, his initial offer: with a few hundred dollars you can live very comfortably in Buenos Aires for several months.

Caught up in the justice system, at the mercy of a shady cop who will keep his file in his personal archives, Mengele returns home exhausted, distressed and desperate. Martha is even more jittery than he is when she throws herself into his arms. She shows him a telegram from Sedlmeier which arrived the previous day, 'Early August, a journalist lodged a formal complaint against you in Ulm.'

A few months ago, Ernst Schnabel published a bestseller, *In the Footsteps of Anne Frank*. He'd investigated the circumstances of her death in Bergen-Belsen and lamented the way so many SS quite simply vanished. 'For example, no one knows what has become of Dr Mengele, the doctor in charge of the selections at Auschwitz. Is he dead or living somewhere?' Several newspapers, notably the *Ulmer Nachrichten*, have published extracts from the book. Ulm is only a short distance – thirty-six kilometres – from Günzburg. In 1958, at the beginning of the summer, the newspaper received an anonymous letter, 'Old Mengele told his former governess that his son, a doctor in the SS, lives in South America . . . The widow of one of his other sons has joined him there.' The newspaper editor sent the letter to Schnabel, who sent it on to the attorney general in Ulm, who the previous year had sentenced to nine years' imprisonment certain members of Einsatzgruppe A who had been active in Lithuania.

Having received a formal complaint, the magistrate asked Günzburg police for information, and those officers hastened to alert the Mengele clan.

34.

Mengele shoves Martha aside violently and hurls the plates from the dinner table at the wall. He is yelling like a madman, a snarling fox, eyes bloodshot and bulging as they were that time in Auschwitz when he spotted twins on the selection ramp. Martha no longer recognises him and backs away. He throws the cutlery, the glasses, a candlestick, everything that is within reach, and heads up to their room, where he stuffs some things into a sports bag – wads of cash, his passport – and leaps into the car. He speeds off without even a backward glance. He could tear his hair out: how damned naïve of him, how presumptuous! What a fool he was, a total prick. He had mocked Eichmann for hiding behind a pseudonym, and there he is: listed in the directory under his own name. A child could smoke him out! Mengele nearly runs over a couple of peacocks as he rockets north, heading for Paraguay, where he can hide. He reassures himself: with a little luck everything will calm down, the abortions, the journalist's formal complaint; his family is powerful, everything and everyone can be bought, just name your price. There is not yet a warrant out for his arrest.

Mengele takes up residence in Asunción. Von Eckstein and Jung welcome him; Sedlmeier and Alois come to him. Karl Sr is old and tired now, so it is the youngest of the brothers who holds the reins of the multinational. The three men talk for a very long time and ask Rudel his advice. A confidant of Stroessner's and a privileged go-between for the Paraguayan army, to which he sells weapons, the pilot pacifies the fugitive. Stroessner's Paraguay is Perón's Argentina. There is nothing to fear. Land can be bought. The country may be chaotic and corrupt, but it is stable, and no one will come looking for him. Whey-faced, Mengele grinds his teeth, 'No, not now!' He has rebuilt his life in Buenos Aires, he has a superb house, his pharmaceutical company is a success. Alois and Sedlmeier encourage him not to rush; thousands of complaints are filed each year, and most do not end in a prosecution. As he is in Paraguay, they entrust him with a new mission: to sell a fertiliser spreader that is hugely successful in Europe.

Mengele deals with country bumpkins, potholed roads and the feverish heat of Chaco. But he has lost heart. A dull anxiety gnaws at him, a dark foreboding: his life is about to go belly up yet again. As he drives, he thinks of the painting in the Alte Pinakothek in Munich that terrified him as a child: Jonah in the mouth of the whale, the prophet about to be swallowed by the sea monster. His friends find him changed, prematurely aged. The dashing intellectual they so admired has become a taciturn and irascible man. One afternoon, he insults Jung's son as he recites his biology lesson. At the poolside *soirées* arranged by his friends he nibbles a few canapés while standing to one side, evasive and tormented. When von Eckstein tries to talk to him, Mengele just smiles nervously. He finds peace of mind only with Haase, Martha and Karl-Heinz, who visit him regularly during the last months of 1958. His nephew proves himself to be a kind, comforting and intelligent son, who deserves to have the reproduction of Dürer's engraving that Mengele was given for his fortieth birthday. Christmas and New Year are celebrated as a family with the Jungs. The Nazis drink toasts: 1959 will be a vintage year. Mengele touches wood. His visa has expired, so he decides to return to Buenos Aires.

35.

He doesn't know it yet, but another detective is on his trail. Hermann Langbein, an Austrian Communist and a veteran of the Spanish Civil War, was a prisoner in Dachau and Auschwitz, where he was forced to act as personal secretary to Eduard Wirths, the camp's chief doctor. Langbein has never forgotten Dr Mengele and has never believed in his disappearance. He picked up his scent by chance when he came across the legal announcement of his divorce in 1954. Two years before that, he co-founded the International Auschwitz Committee to fight for compensation for concentration camp survivors and to gather testimonies so that they could take their torturers to court. Patiently, discreetly, Langbein investigates Mengele, accumulating evidence against him. He feels sure that he lives in Buenos Aires, having noted the Argentine lawyer's involvement in divorce proceedings. Langbein passes on the case files to the German federal minister of justice, who declares the case outside his jurisdiction: Mengele should be tried by a regional court. Most of the judges refuse to act, but in Freiburg im Breisgau – Mengele's last registered address, from the time he helped Irene settle there at the end of the war – the prosecutor issues an arrest warrant, on 25 February 1959, for multiple cases of premeditated murder and attempted murder. Langbein does not give up: since Mengele is living in Buenos Aires, the Ministry of Foreign Affairs must demand his extradition by the Argentine government.

Sedlmeier sends a telegram to Mengele with this news, given to him by one of his police informants. Stalling is now out of the question. He must sell the villa and his shares in Fadro Farm, close his bank accounts and take refuge in Paraguay. It is by no means certain that the new democratically elected, liberal Argentine government will be as lenient towards the Nazis as its Perónist and military predecessors. Buenos Aires may well give in to the request from Bonn. Mengele is distraught, on the verge of a breakdown, as he packs his scientific journals in a cardboard box and without explanation bids farewell to his partners in the pharmaceutical laboratory. Martha and Karl-Heinz can stay in Argentina but will have to move; great discretion is required. He kisses them and says they will meet 'soon' in Asunción.

Once again, Rudel comes to the rescue, who will help him acquire Paraguayan citizenship: no Extradition Treaty binds Bonn and Asunción. President Stroessner will never deliver one of Paraguay's nationals to a foreign power; Paraguayan sovereignty is sacred. Overwhelmed by the idea of being in a big city, Mengele begs his friend to find him a place to hide in the countryside, in a German community. Obliging as ever, Rudel turns to Alban Krug, a florid Nazi with the build of a wrestler who owns a farm in the Nueva Bavaria enclave, a few kilometres from the Argentine border.

36.

Life moves at a slow pace in the German town of Hohenau in southern Paraguay. Its buildings fan out around the church square, where canny but superstitious Guarani Indians pass the time. In the red-earth streets, cows and pigs slop about, swarms of insects swirl around stalls selling sausages and snakeskins, and blond children steer oxcarts to the Paraná River down below. The European settlers work their fingers to the bone in fields of corn and watermelons beneath an overpowering sun, their hair soaked with sweat. The sluggish rhythm of village life is accompanied by the singing of hummingbirds. The autumn beer festival is a welcome distraction, and the southern spring is fêted with a banquet at which drunken rural labourers engage in line or circle dancing, like a painting by Bruegel the Elder, four centuries ago. Mengele nervously watches them.

Loyal, gluttonous and uneducated, Alban Krug reminds him of his dog, Heinrich Lyons. Mengele's protector is vaguely in charge of a farm cooperative, but the farm's accounts suggest that Krug prefers the beer produced by one of his associates, his wife's invigorating cuisine, and hunting and fishing with his son Oskar and his daughters. The farmer brushes off the modern management methods that his lodger tries to teach him. Mengele continues to work as a traveling salesman, roaming all over Paraguay with only a catalogue of agricultural machinery and his tortured thoughts for company. He swears and fulminates, angry about having lost his Argentine cocoon, moaning about his fate, fretting about being caught or having to live indefinitely in hiding at that fool Krug's place. Anxiety attacks are occasionally followed by tentative optimism. If he obtains Paraguayan citizenship, he will be able to rebuild his life, buy land and settle down with Karl-Heinz and Martha, although it will be difficult to convince his wife to come. She is his greatest worry: instead of supporting him, she says she cannot cope with the heat, the power cuts, the red dust which gets in everywhere – 'Hohenau and the Paraguayan country-side are not to Madame's liking.' He should have slapped her when she collapsed in tears after being bitten by a spider the first night she arrived. She isn't suited to a fugitive's life, constantly on the move, sleeping in hotels. It's his fault for spoiling her; he got her used to a different standard of living. She complains bitterly about his absences. Their acquaintances in Buenos Aires keep asking for news and she does not know what to say; as for Karl-Heinz, he's been unsettled ever since his father's departure. If they move to the jungle, what will they do about his education? A Mengele does not just study *anywhere*. Martha is convinced that Josef is exaggerating. He should come back to Buenos Aires; they could be happy there as they were at first. There's no real risk. She thinks to herself that his brother, Karl Jr, was far braver.

Mengele agrees to meet her in Asunción, where he tries to cut a dashing figure as they dine with the Jungs and von

Eckstein. His life is in their hands; the two men are sponsoring his application for naturalisation, and von Eckstein has introduced him to one of the best lawyers in the country. But the whole enterprise is illegal: to be eligible for citizenship you need to have been resident in Paraguay for five years.

37.

A race against the clock ensues. The demand for Mengele's extradition has been forwarded from Bonn to Buenos Aires, and another one is on its way to Asunción; rumour has it that he has fled to Paraguay. The whole process is lagging in Argentina. Legal obstacles are piling up, wrapped in red tape; Junker, the German ambassador, dithers and procrastinates; the request passes through the Ministry of Foreign Affairs, the president of the Senate, the attorney general, a Federal Court judge, the police, tribunals. The Argentine and West German governments are undisturbed by the colossal muddle. In Paraguay, the Ministry of the Interior and the police know of the upcoming extradition request, since Interpol asked them for a copy of the applicant's naturalisation file, but Rudel intervenes with the minister. His friend, the brilliant Dr José Mengele, is being pursued for his political beliefs in Germany; nothing bad; he will be of great use to Paraguay, so his naturalisation is urgent. In November 1959, it's a done deal. The

Supreme Court of Paraguay gives Mengele citizenship, a residence permit, a certificate of good behaviour and an ID card.

Yet by the time Mengele arrives at the Jungs' home, he is on the verge of collapse. They are throwing a small party to celebrate the good news. His eyes brimming with tears, he stammers that his father just died. Germany has lost a patriot and he has lost an irreplaceable ally, his shield. His fearsome and uncompromising father never dropped him in spite of everything. In Günzburg, an imposing portrait of the deceased is plastered across the façade of the town hall, while thousands of kilometres away Mengele pours out his grief by the garlanded swimming pool in the sultry Asunción night. He describes to von Eckstein, Karl Heinz, Rudel, and the Jung and Haase couples how he climbed the Hirschberg mountain in the summer of 1919 with his father. One rare time back then when just the two of them were together, they had picnicked overlooking the Bavarian lakes sparkling far below like rolls of silvertone film, and a butterfly had landed on his sleeve. When he was a child, before he fell asleep, his fearsome father would recite a Latin prayer learnt from the Trappists after Josef had nearly drowned in a reservoir at the age of six: *Procul recedant somnia et noctium phantasmata.* From all ill dreams defend our sight, from fears and terrors of the night.

Mengele is inconsolable; he stutters and sobs like a little girl. He must go to the funeral and will catch the first plane to Europe next day. Rudel dissuades him: it'd be an act of suicide, the police would arrest him in the cemetery, so he must drop the idea. On the day of the funeral, the undertakers place on the coffin a wreath of flowers with an anonymous message: 'I salute you from afar.'

38.

Eichmann has been spotted in Buenos Aires, where he is now working in a warehouse for Mercedes Benz. Lothar Hermann, a blind German Jewish refugee in Argentina, is convinced that he has tracked him down. For a long time, Hermann's daughter dated Nick Eichmann, who often praised his father's prowess during the war and regretted that Germany did not annihilate all the Jews. In 1957, Hermann writes to Fritz Bauer, the chief public prosecutor in Hesse. Rather than collaborating with the intelligence agencies and the German embassy in Buenos Aires, which is infested with old Nazis, Bauer prefers to give information on the quiet to Mossad. The Israeli intelligence agencies conduct an investigation in Argentina, but it is inconclusive, and Mossad puts a stop to it: Hermann is asking for too much money; the home of the man suspected of being the great exterminator of the Jews of Europe is a rathole in the suburbs of Buenos Aires. Unthinkable. But Bauer believes Hermann's allegations. He tracks down a second source that corroborates his story: Ricardo Klement is Adolf Eichmann. This time Mossad intervenes. In December 1959, the decision is made to kidnap the Nazi SS officer.

Isser Harel, the director of Mossad, is secretly plotting a second kidnapping: he dreams of pinning the name Mengele to his investigation board. West Germany's demand for extradition was leaked in the press, and the World Jewish Congress encourages the survivors of Auschwitz to testify to his heinous crimes before Langbein. Harel has only scattered and dated information: Mengele goes by the name of Gregor, he runs a furniture factory in the centre of Buenos Aires. Harel's plan is simple: after Eichmann's arrest, set for 11 May 1960, his men will have nine days to get their hands on the Nazi doctor and bring him to the plane flying Eichmann back to Israel.

Since becoming a citizen of Paraguay and receiving some of his legacy from his father, Mengele is doing all he can to eliminate his dark thoughts. He goes water-skiing, researches the Guayaki Indians with the eccentric von Eckstein and is once again viewing his future with a certain amount of serenity. There are fewer tensions with Martha, and he can move around more freely. At the beginning of 1960, while underground units of Mossad plan the kidnapping of Eichmann in Buenos Aires, he spends several days at the guesthouse in the neighbourhood of Vicente López where his wife is staying with Karl-Heinz. A few weeks later, in April, they are in Hotel Tirol, a luxurious establishment in Encarnación in southern Paraguay. The indefatigable Sedlmeier has joined them. They discuss money, methods of communication and how best to develop their subsidiary company in Paraguay. Mengele shows his partner photos of a beautiful property he wants to buy in the Alto Paraná region. He goes back to Krug reassured, almost happy,

Martha having finally accepted the idea of following him into exile.

In early May, Operation Attila enters its active phase with the arrival of Mossad commandos in Buenos Aires. Harel has slipped Mengele's coded file into his luggage. On the 11th, as planned, Eichmann is seized. In the hideout where they have locked him up, the Israeli agents interrogate him: Does he know Mengele? Where is he hiding? What does he look like now? What are his habits in Buenos Aires? Whom does he see? 'Eichmann, where is Mengele?' The Nazi is like a man of stone. Despite their differences, despite his contempt for Mengele, he refuses point-blank to betray his comrade-in-arms: 'Loyalty is my badge of honour.' The Israelis persevere, make promises, threaten, insist, and finally Eichmann gives them the address of the Vicente López guesthouse.

Time is running out. But the Israelis move carefully, because the Nazis of Buenos Aires are on the alert. As soon as their father's disappearance is discovered, Eichmann's sons race to see Sassen to coordinate a search. They are convinced it's a Jewish plot and plan to blow up the Israeli embassy or kidnap the ambassador in retaliation. They scour the city with the help of Tacuara Nationalist militia and Perónist Youth; Sassen is responsible for keeping watch on the airport.

Harel sends two agents to the guesthouse, an isolated villa surrounded by a palisade at the end of a narrow street. It is difficult to watch it without being seen. The manageress does not know a man by the name of Gregor or Mengele. A postman is more talkative: a Mengele family lived there, but disappeared a few weeks ago, without leaving a forwarding address. At the furniture factory, no one has ever heard of a German called Gregor. The days go by; the doctor, exiled in Paraguay, is nowhere to be found, but Harel refuses to give up. The name Mengele 'burns like fire in his bones', and the Mossad chief contemplates raiding the pension, certain that the Nazi has returned, but his men dissuade him. The entire operation could go belly up.

On 20 May 1960, an El Al plane flies out of Buenos Aires, bound for Tel Aviv with Adolf Eichmann on board, drugged and dressed as a member of the air crew. Harel swears to his men that they will soon have Mengele's guts for garters. They will create a new special unit with tracking down Nazis its mission. The Auschwitz doctor will be their first target.

39.

A few days later, when Israeli prime minister David Ben-Gurion announces the capture of Eichmann to the Knesset, the Nazi war criminals in South America are aghast. Who is next on the list? Who will be kidnapped, beaten, shot in cold blood in his bed or in a parking lot by a commando unit of avengers who suddenly materialise out of nowhere? Who will be forcibly extradited to Israel and exposed to the vengeance of the Jews and world opinion in a degrading glass cage, like a monster in a fairground sideshow, as Eichmann is during his trial in Jerusalem the following year? Nazis in exile no longer have peace of mind. If they want to save their skins, they must become outlaws, renounce their fleshpot pleasures and be condemned to a clandestine fugitive existence, with nowhere to hide or to rest.

The hunt for Nazi war criminals is now open. Journalists from around the world head to Buenos Aires to pursue their own investigations. Eichmann's kidnapping heralds a new era. It is a humiliation for Argentina and a disaster for West Germany. The former nation must prove that it is not a Nazi sanctuary. On 20 June, a warrant for Mengele's arrest is issued. It will lead, the following year, to the capture of . . . Lothar Hermann, wrongly accused of being the Auschwitz doctor. Now West Germany must prove she is ready to judge her criminals and face her past. At last, the great clean-up operation begins. Nazi groups in Buenos Aires fall apart. Sassen's friends suspect him of betraying Eichmann, and he sells the recorded interviews for a mint to *Life* magazine and the German and Dutch media too, before fleeing to Uruguay, where he introduces himself as a 'reformed Nazi'.

'That pretentious prick Eichie and his damned hubris!' Mengele explodes with anger in Krug's kitchen as he hears about Eichmann's kidnapping on the radio. He vituperates against the accursed Jews, the incompetent Argentines, the venal Germans, the entire planet. When Krug tells him that he has nothing to fear, because he only obeyed orders and looked after people in the camps, he wants to shoot him between his eyes, see him and all his family slumped over the dinner table. He would do them all in, one after the other, the girls last of all – 'on your knees, you silly goose'. The Krugs would take it in the neck for all the Jews, the Argentines, the Germans, the whole wide world, and as for that son of a bitch Eichmann, that one, if only he could bump him off in his Israeli cell and then disappear into the jungle, forever. But Mengele starts to shake; his hands, his arms, his legs tremble and threaten to give way. Krug's mother makes him sit down and drink some sugared water. When he comes back to his senses, he faces the usual odious reality: he is sure to drown in the well into which Eichmann's capture has plunged him. Eichmann is likely to turn him in to the Israelis. Others will blab; he has left traces everywhere, his papers are in his name, and there's his wife and son. It will be easy to follow his trail to this farm, which lies open to the elements, with just Krug, an old Walther pistol and a few pitchforks for defence against Mossad's seasoned hitmen. So Mengele is constantly on the move; he does not feel safe anywhere. Day and night he chews at his moustache and goes round in circles like a wasp trapped in a glass, threatened with asphyxiation. When he finally falls asleep, at around three or four in the morning, several hours after taking some sleeping tablets, the slightest sound, the creaking floor, an insignificant insect, jolt him awake. He is fearful of being recognised now that the West German government has put a price on his head of 20,000 marks. He has (finally) become world-famous. The press details his atrocities alongside his photograph.

Rolf now knows that his father did not disappear in Russia, but is the Auschwitz 'Angel of Death'. Mengele tries to justify himself to his friends in Asunción, to play down his role, but people steer clear of him. Jung escapes and returns to Germany, and only von Eckstein believes him. The fugitive is fearful; he suffers and moans. His loyal friend Haase, who regularly sent him poetry collections and wrote telling him not to lose his nerve, but to resist and stand firm, has just died, falling off a ladder in Buenos Aires.

In September 1960, Mengele decides that he has to disappear, to flee, leave everything behind him and reinvent himself, at age forty-nine, otherwise the Israelis will catch him. Mossad's special unit monitors the comings and goings of his wife and son and is getting dangerously close to Krug's farm. Rudel gives him a Mauser pistol and a new Brazilian ID card in the name of Peter Hochbichler. Mengele must separate from Martha and Karl-Heinz; they return to Europe without saying goodbye to him. He hurriedly burns his notes and his German passport and destroys his Auschwitz specimens. At dawn, one clear October morning, Krug and Rudel drive him to the Brazilian border in a jeep. As the strapping Krug yells to him that his war is not yet over, Mengele does not turn around, and is swallowed up by the emerald-green jungle foliage.

He is marked by the curse of Cain, the first human to commit murder: a fugitive, doomed to wander the earth, and to be killed by anyone who finds him.

PART II

The Rat

*The punishment matches the guilt: to be deprived of
all appetite for life, to be brought to the highest degree
of weariness of life.*

Søren Kierkegaard

40.

At the Tinguely Museum in Basel, there is a room submerged in darkness. The atmosphere is one of carnage, like an abandoned torture chamber. A monstrous altarpiece featuring a hippopotamus skull is surrounded by machine sculptures made of animal carcasses, charred wooden beams, fire-twisted metals: materials recovered by the artist Jean Tinguely from the rubble of a burned-out farmhouse struck by lightning near the Swiss village where he had his studio. Among the carbonised remains is the skeleton of a large Mengele threshing machine.

Under a black sun, the machine sculptures are set in motion. Wheels, pulleys and chains grind and squeal, discordant, as in a marshalling yard. The steel jaws gape; human and animal skulls move along a conveyor belt while their shadows whirl across the walls like immense syringes, executioners' axes, saws, hammers, scythes, gallows. This shrieking waltz is a macabre contrast to the rest of the museum, which hums with jazz, the pale green-and-blue reflections of the Rhine shimmering through the bay windows. Here, amid the heavy-metal cacophony, the machine sculptures threaten to whip and slash you, to capture you and escort you onto the ramp. Haunted by death and concentration camps, Tinguely created this work and called it *Mengele-danse macabre*.

In the summer and autumn of 1944, one Hungarian prisoner was forced to learn the steps to that dance of death. Miklós Nyiszli was a doctor and belonged to the Sonderkommandos, the living dead conscripted to harvest hair and gold from the gassed corpses before throwing them into the ovens. Nyiszli, a Jew himself, was Mengele's scalpel. Following orders, he would saw through the top of the skull, cut open the thorax, slice through the pericardium. After his miraculous escape from hell, he recorded these unimaginable horrors in a book, *Auschwitz: A Doctor's Eyewitness Account*, published in Hungary in 1946, and in France in 1961.

'Dr Mengele, chief physician of K.Z. Auschwitz, is indefatigable in the exercise of his duties. He spends long hours immersed in his work. He stands half the day on the Judenrampe, where four to five trainloads of deported Hungarians arrive per day . . . His arm moves in only one direction. To the left! And so entire trainloads go, without exception, into the gas chambers or onto the pyres . . . He considers the dispatch of hundreds of thousands of Jews to the gas chambers to be a patriotic duty.'

In the experimental barracks of the Gypsy camp, 'We perform on twins and dwarves every medical test that can be done on living humans. Blood tests, spinal taps, blood transfusions between twins, and innumerable other tests, all of them painful, exhausting and *in vivo*.' For the 'simultaneous evaluation of detected anomalies, the twins have to die at the same time! And die they do, in an experimental barracks of

K.Z. Auschwitz, in Sector BIII of the camp, by the hand of Dr Mengele.'

Injections of chloroform are administered to the heart. The organs are shipped by mail to the Institute for Anthropology, Human Heredity and Eugenics in Dahlem, Berlin, of which Professor von Verschuer is the director. In order to ensure that the 'scientifically interesting parts' are transmitted promptly, the package is stamped with the words 'Urgent, important war material'.

'Dr Mengele is considered to be a great representative of German medical science . . . The work he does in the dissection hall is performed in the service of German medicine.'

When scarlet fever broke out in the barracks occupied by Hungarian Jews, Mengele made arrangements: the 'trucks arrived and took the inhabitants of all three barracks to the crematorium'.

Nyiszli is haunted by the macabre aura of his torturer: 'His cheerful face hides so much cruelty . . . To find so much cynicism mixed with so much evil in a doctor surprised me, even in the camp . . . The name "Dr Mengele" worked like magic. Just hearing it uttered was enough to make most people tremble.'

Nyiszli describes Mengele's manic zeal in the crematorium dissection room, even in autumn 1944 when Germany has already lost the war: 'At the usual hour, around five in the afternoon, Dr Mengele arrives . . . He sits for long hours beside me among the microscopes, flasks and test tubes, or stands for long hours at the dissecting table in a blood-stained lab coat, with bloody hands, and examines and researches like one possessed . . . Just the other day it happened that I was sitting at my laboratory table with him. We were leafing through the dossiers of the twins processed so far when he noticed a faint grease stain on the light-blue cardboard cover of one of them . . . He looked at me reproachfully and asked quite seriously, "How can you be so careless with these dossiers which I have so lovingly collected?"'

Nyiszli's daily routine is insane. 'The blazing flames of the pyres send their light all the way here. The smoke from the chimneys of the four crematoria is pervasive. The air is heavy with the smell of burning human flesh and singed hair. The screams of those going to their deaths and the explosive reports of shots to the back of the neck make the building's walls tremble. Dr Mengele returns here after every selection and bloody fireworks display. He spends all his free time here in this atmosphere of horrors, and with a silent fury he makes me open up the corpses of hundreds of innocents sent to their deaths. Bacteria propagates itself in the electric incubator on a growth medium prepared from human flesh. He sits before the microscope for hours at a time and looks for the cause of phenomena such as none will ever decipher, the cause of multiple births.'

41.

One day two Jews from Lódź ghetto, a hunchbacked father and his crippled son, arrive in one of the transports. When Mengele spots them on the ramp waiting for the selection to begin, he takes them out of line and sends them to Crematorium I to be examined by Nyiszli. The Hungarian doctor takes their measurements and gives them meat stew and macaroni, their 'last supper', he writes. Oberscharführer Mussfeldt and four Sonderkommandos take the pair away, strip them and shoot them at close range as ordered by Mengele. The corpses are brought back to Nyiszli, who 'feels nausea at the horror of it' and entrusts the autopsies to his companions.

'In the evening, after he has sent at least 10,000 people to their deaths in this one day, Dr Mengele arrives. He listens with great interest to my report on the two physically defective victims *in vivo* and to the subsequent autopsy data. "These corpses must not be cremated," he says. "They will be prepared and the skeletons will go to the anthropological institute in Dahlem, Berlin." He asks me what methods I know for the perfect cleaning of skeletons. "I know two methods," I reply. "One is the dissolving method, which consists of placing the corpse in a calcium chloride solution; within two weeks this will burn away all soft parts. After that the bones go into a gasoline bath, which dissolves the fat off them, thereby leaving them dry, odourless and snow-white in colour. The second method, the cooking method, is shorter. It consists of simply cooking the body in water until the fleshy parts are easily and smoothly removable from the bones. Afterwards, here too we employ a gasoline bath for the degreasing and bleaching of the bones.'

Dr Mengele orders Nyiszli to use the faster method: cooking. The stoves are built from bricks in the courtyard, the tinplate barrels are placed over them, and the corpses of the hunchbacked father and crippled son, two humble Jews from Lódź, simmer for five hours. 'After repeated tests, I ascertain that the soft parts separate easily from the bones. I put out the fires, but the barrels will remain in place until cooled.'

That day, the crematorium is not operating; four stone-mason prisoners are repairing its chimney. One of Nyiszli's men rushes up to him, quite beside himself. 'Doctor, the Poles are eating the flesh from the barrels!' He leaps from his seat and runs to the courtyard, where four unfamiliar prisoners in striped clothing are standing, immobile, around the barrels. The Polish stonemasons having completed their work were waiting for their guards to take them back to their quarters in Auschwitz I. Half-starved, they searched about for something to eat and came across the barrels, left unguarded for a few minutes. They assumed that the meat cooking in the big barrels was for the Sonderkommandos. They were almost paralysed with terror when they learnt what kind of flesh they had eaten.

Mengele is very satisfied with the skeletons laid out on the laboratory table. 'He brought with him several high-ranking medical colleagues to examine the skeletons. They fiddled self-importantly with a few pieces and tossed around scientific terms. They behaved as if the deformities in the skeletons of the two victims were unparalleled medical findings . . . The two skeletons are packed into long, sturdy paper bags, and will travel in this manner to Berlin with the accompanying data. On to this shipment also went the "Urgent, important war shipment" stamp.'

Mengele is the Prince of European darkness. The arrogant doctor dissected, tortured and burned children. The son of a prosperous family sent 400,000 human beings to the gas chamber as he whistled. For a long time he thought he could get out of it easily, he who was 'the little runt born of mud and fire' and saw himself become a demi-god, he who flouted laws and commandments and inflicted unfeelingly so much suffering and pain on his fellow men, his brothers.

Europe, valley of tears.

Europe, necropolis of a civilisation annihilated by Mengele and the henchmen of the Black Order with their skull insignias, the poisoned tip of an arrow released in 1914.

Mengele, model employee of the death factory, the mass murderer who thought he could escape punishment.

But now he is cornered, a prisoner of his own existence, a modern Cain wandering through Brazil.

Thus begins the doctor's descent into hell. He will gnaw at his own heart; he will lose himself in the dark night.

42.

Mengele is grumbling as he approaches the bathroom mirror, a towel tied around his waist. The bluish tinge of the dark, puffy circles under his eyes contrasts with the pallor of his face, his thin chest and sagging pecs. How he has aged, these last months! He pinches his lips and chews at his moustache, which is like a grey, grubby doormat, so un-intellectual, albeit Germanic, he thinks; when he eats soup he licks it as an old cat licks his whiskers. It disgusts him, though it partially camouflages the space between his two upper front teeth, which comforts him. Almost nothing else reassures him any more since his arrival in Brazil a year ago. This morning of 7 October 1961, he is even more anxious than usual; a big knot is torturing his stomach. He automatically massages his temples upwards in front of the mirror, as though the friction could dissipate his pain and soothe his prominent forehead; that accursed forehead which has always bothered him and which will eventually be his undoing, along with the space between his front teeth, which Irene warned him about fifteen years ago.

Mengele closes his eyes. He who believes in nothing clenches his fists and repeats Rudel's mantra in a low voice: 'He who abandons himself is lost.' He must get a move on, shave and brush his teeth, put on his linen trousers, his shoes, button his cream-coloured shirt to the neck – it is already too hot for a tie – and adjust the position of his wide-brimmed hat, which rarely leaves his head. Mengele grabs two suitcases and descends from the first floor. A smiling man waiting at the foot of the stairs takes his luggage and packs it into the boot of a modest Ford Anglia. They leave the city, Itapecerica, a little before 8 a.m.

The obliging man wearing dark glasses is Wolfgang Gerhard, the São Paulo representative for Rudel's Kameradenwerk. The flying ace had contacted him as soon as he had decided to exfiltrate Mengele to Brazil. The family in Günzburg was sceptical to begin with: Gerhard has been struggling since leaving Austria in 1949, so won't he massively overcharge? How can they trust an individual who sings in a choir and has a fondness for alcohol? Their informants are adamant on this point. Rudel is reassuring: Gerhard will not demand a pfennig; to protect a war criminal of Mengele's rank is an honour, a priceless commitment for him; he is a fanatical Nazi. His son's name is Adolf. He dreams of tying Simon Wiesenthal's corpse to the bumper of his car and dragging it down the street like tin cans on a wedding day. Gerhard's Christmas tree is topped by a swastika.

As his driver snakes north, Mengele stares at the hairy paws grasping the steering wheel and the legs too long for the Ford's footwell. Gerhard reminds him of a teenager clambering onto a merry-go-round for children, keen to impress his friends who doubted his daring. Gerhard is whistling. It is a great day for a man who was only twenty at the end of the war, who prints propaganda and anti-Semitic scandal sheets that usually go unnoticed. His mission is one worthy of the elite soldier that he could have been had the forces of evil not united against Nazism: to take the famous Dr Mengele to the sanctuary that he – little Gerhard, a rookie – found personally, on the road to an isolated farm near Nova Europa, 300 kilometres from São Paulo. The place is owned by a couple of Hungarians, Geza and Gitta Stammer. They left their country after the war because of the Soviet invasion. Gerhard met them a few years earlier at a gathering of Central European expatriates. They are humble people and politically sound; they will not be problematic.

As the landscape becomes increasingly arid, Mengele's anxiety increases. For the umpteenth time, Gerhard has to describe his plan, which has received Rudel's blessing and that of Mengele's family in Günzburg. The Austrian is used to having to reassure the fugitive. When Mengele first landed in Brazil, Gerhard employed him in his confectionary shop; comforting and encouraging him like a son. For Gerhard, dedicating himself to Mengele is akin to saving Berlin from the flames: a duty that is its own reward. His business, his wife and two children have been of secondary importance over the past year.

Gerhard will introduce Mengele to the Stammer couple as Peter Hochbichler, a Swiss livestock-breeding specialist who no longer wants to live alone at fifty. Eccentric Hochbichler is coming out of a tricky period, Gerhard has told them. He has had health problems and is looking for companionship and work. And he has just inherited a tidy sum and would like to invest it by buying land. As Geza is a surveyor, he is often absent for long periods, and Hochbichler can manage their farm. The

Stammers are not well off and have accepted Gerhard's proposal. They will not pay Hochbichler, but he will be fed, housed, concealed.

The road becomes a single track and then deteriorates into a dusty lane that snakes through the savannah to an old farm. Final stop: dogs bark and jump up at the car, and a forty-year-old couple appears with two sons on the threshold of the wooden house. The Stammer family is impatient to meet its mysterious benefactor, Peter Hochbichler.

43.

Travelling under the protection of a praetorian guard of Indians in March 1961, Mengele is identified in the small town of Mato Grosso, but manages to escape the ambush plotted by the Brazilian police. Some months later he is reported arrested in the state of Minas Gerais, in southeastern Brazil. This turns out to be an unfortunate mistake: the man detained is identified as an ex-Waffen SS member on holiday. Mengele is spotted once again in February 1962, this time in a town on the border with Paraguay. His hotel is stormed by an elite military police unit, but he left that very morning. The Argentine press announces that he murdered a Mossad agent in Bariloche. Armed and extremely dangerous, he has a private army in his pay, which accompanies him wherever he goes.

Since a reward has been put on his head and the nature of his crimes fully revealed, Mengele is a subject of fantasy and conjecture. He is becoming a mythical creature; 'the diabolical doctor, Satan's henchman, not comparable to a man despite his appearance', playwright Rolf Hochhuth writes in *The Deputy: A Christian Tragedy* in 1963.

Mossad is not sidetracked by the wild rumours. The special unit has its headquarters in Paris, headed by Zvi Aharoni, a German Jew instrumental in the kidnapping of Eichmann, who swears he will drag his compatriot before an Israeli court. He has accurate information and has identified two of Mengele's contacts in South America: Krug and Rudel. But the hunt is complex, the family and its entourage in Günzburg are impenetrable, and Krug's family is suspicious – one of the girls resists the playboy allure of the special-unit agent sent to charm her. Aharoni deploys several more agents in Paraguay, convinced that Mengele has returned there; the Israelis have got wind of his naturalisation. Rudel is tailed all over South America, and Martha's mail is intercepted. Aharoni tries to infiltrate the German community's institutions in Asunción. Mossad is turning up the heat, but not yet to boiling point. Mengele is still one step ahead.

That is, until the spring of 1962. In Uruguay, Aharoni has hunted down some big game with the sort of deeply personal knowledge spymasters can only dream of. Sassen comes forward, prepared to traduce his old friend Mengele, ostensibly because he has sullied the honour of the SS but principally because Sassen needs money to support his glitzy, luxurious lifestyle – and all his mistresses. Mossad greases his palm handsomely. The Dutch adventurer has lost track of Mengele, but soon finds out that he has fled to Brazil and identifies his new protector, Wolfgang Gerhard, the fugitive's only contact with the outside world. The Mossad agents do not let go of Gerhard. And one morning, the Austrian's Ford Anglia takes off into the savannah, bound for an isolated farm.

Aharoni goes for a picnic in the vicinity of the farm with two agents who are Brazilian Jews. Three men come to meet them. One of them is of medium build and looks European; he has a moustache and a hat pressed down firmly over his eyes. He keeps quiet and stands back while his two beefy companions speak Portuguese with the three walkers. Aharoni lets his men do the talking while he observes the man in the hat, who avoids his gaze. It's him: he'd bet his life on it. God, he would love to get his hands around that throat and crush the life out of it, but he keeps his cool. Another unit must come to take photos of the man to make certain. Just a few weeks more . . . The worst thing would be to arouse the suspicions of the suspect. The three men return to the farm, and Aharoni goes back to his Parisian headquarters, where he begins work on an operation even trickier than Eichmann's kidnapping.

44.

On his return to France, a surprise awaits Aharoni in his office. An emaciated and unusually nervous Isser Harel, the director of Mossad, instructs him to suspend the hunt for Mengele in order to devote himself to tracking down an eight-year-old child. Police suspect his maternal grandfather, an ultra-Orthodox Jew, of having kidnapped him. In Israel, little Yossele had been entrusted to him by his parents, secular Jews who were experiencing great financial difficulties. When they came to fetch their boy, the grandfather explained that Yossele had to be raised according to the prescriptions of the Torah and would not be returned. On their second visit, the boy had vanished. When the grandfather was locked up for refusing to cooperate with the police, enraged religious extremists took to the streets and started to throw stones: the Jewish state has locked up an old man, a holy man, they cry. 'Ben-Gurion is a Nazi!' Israel is on the verge of civil war as Orthodox and secular citizens curse and polish their weapons. Prime Minister Ben-Gurion risks losing his majority in the Knesset at the next election. Yossele must be found in order to appease social tensions. Since the child is probably abroad by now, Mossad needs to intervene and set its forty best sleuths on his trail; it is a prime ministerial order. Aharoni is mobilised and Operation Tiger put into action.

The officer pinches himself but obeys. With Mengele cornered, he and his team now have to wear false beards to infiltrate the most extreme Judaic cults in Europe, the United States and South America. Nazi hunters find themselves blackmailing rabbis in Pigalle brothels, photographs in hand. Finally, they pick up a scent: Yossele has been kidnapped by a French aristocrat, a convert to Judaism and a heroine of the Resistance, Madeleine Frei, who is infatuated with the Guardians of the City, the grandfather's sect. It is a fantastic story: Frei dyed the boy's hair blond and dressed him in girl's clothes to get him out of Israeli jurisdiction. Yossele is found living with an ultra-Orthodox family in Brooklyn and is brought back to Israel. Operation Tiger has lasted eight months and cost Mossad $1 million. Meanwhile, Mengele has moved.

45.

His acclimatisation a year ago was difficult. Mengele arrived in Nova Europa at the beginning of the dry season. It had never been so hot than at the end of that year, 1961. With no rain before Christmas, the nights were more suffocating than at Krug's place in Hohenau. The work was gruelling and the soil arid. The Stammers lived on their smallholding as if it were still the Middle Ages, with no telephone or electricity.

Gitta, the farmer's wife, watched Peter Hochbichler closely on the coffee plantation. He started work at dawn and left the fields later than the other farm workers. He was industrious and fussed over the cows, hens, mare and three pigs in stables that stank of dung, whistling Mozart and Puccini. After one month, the Stammers, or rather Gitta, since Geza only came home some weekends, decided to accept and keep on the needy yet strangely narcissistic labourer. Every morning, before leaving for the fields, Hochbichler splashed himself with eau de Cologne and looked at himself languidly in the entrance-hall mirror. He wore a hat the whole time, and pulled it over his face as soon as he was approached. Despite the overwhelming heat, he had on heavy boots and a lab coat buttoned up to the neck, a white gabardine overgarment that made him look like a site foreman responsible for filling silos with grain. His hands were odd: the palms and knuckles were calloused like those of a manual labourer, but his nails were manicured as if he were a member of Budapest's upper classes. He washed them thirty times a day and rubbed his forearms vigorously with black soap as a surgeon disinfects himself before performing surgery.

Hochbichler was a weird old bird: he ate tidily and spoke gently but knew how to make blood pudding. A few days before Christmas, he smashed in the skull of a pig with an axe and sliced its throat with a fearsome knife, which he had sharpened the previous day. He collected the gush of blood and whipped it up, stirring it with his arms up to the elbows in a big bowl to prevent it from clotting. Then, working like a madman, he had scoured the insides of the animal, removing the lungs, kidneys, liver and fatty intestines. The Stammers, their workers and families feasted on it all on New Year's Eve.

One morning when he was out in the fields, Gitta went into his room, which he had, unusually, forgotten to lock. She searched through his things, and in addition to the carefully folded designer clothes she found an English umbrella, hundreds of dollars in wads of high-denomination bank notes, newspapers and scientific journals in Spanish and German, a large padlocked notebook, classified papers that she did not dare to try to decipher, opera recordings, and books by unfamiliar authors – Heidegger, Carl Schmitt, Novalis, Heinrich von Treitschke. She was only a little surprised when she discovered Hochbichler's true identity by chance. On Saturday, 27 January 1962, Geza brought back a leading broadsheet from São Paulo. To commemorate the seventeenth anniversary of the liberation of Auschwitz concentration camp, there was a photo of a triumphant young SS doctor nicknamed the 'Angel of Death', a certain Josef Mengele, still on the run. The portrait caught Gitta's eye. She noted the doctor's piercing gaze, his diabolical eyebrows, the gap between his two front teeth, his slightly domed forehead. She asked her eldest son Roberto to fetch Hochbichler and showed him the picture. Trembling, paler than a death, he left the room without saying a word.

The same evening, after the meal he had barely touched, the Swiss farmer confessed to the Stammers that 'unfortunately' he was Mengele, but that he did not commit the crimes of which 'the press under instructions from the Jews' accused him.

46.

True or false, the Stammers did not care about all the Mengele stories, or about Auschwitz. Geza had studied in Germany during the war; neither he nor his future wife had been bothered by the deportation of Jews from Hungary, or by the massacres perpetrated at the end of 1944 by Arrow Cross militiamen on the banks of the frozen River Danube, which carried away the bodies of Jews, Gypsies and the opponents of the Szálasi regime, which they supported. They, too, had suffered. Their parents in Transylvania had lost their lands after the 1918 defeat, and one of Gitta's sisters had been raped and murdered by Red Army soldiers invading Hungary. Since then, their motherland had been occupied by the Soviets, who had forced them to emigrate and to stagnate in this rathole. They were indifferent to charges brought by a Brazilian broadsheet against the German doctor. But they wanted peace.

They could not sleep that night. Their Swiss farm labourer was one of the most wanted war criminals in the world, with a reward on his head offered by the government of Federal Germany. Geza was in a panic. He went round and round their room in circles, newspaper in hand like a flaming torch. The author of the article confirmed, via a reliable source, that Israel was preparing to kidnap Mengele in South America, using the same avenging commandos who had kidnapped Eichmann in Argentina. Mossad would storm the farm and murder their little boys. They had to ditch their guest as soon as possible. Geza would delay his departure for São Paulo and get in touch with Gerhard.

The Austrian did his best to reassure the Hungarian: nobody knew where Mengele was hiding, the newspapers wrote whatever they liked, the Stammers were not at risk. They should be proud of hosting a pre-eminent scientist of the Third Reich, and of fulfilling a mission crucial to a cause that would eventually triumph. For anonymous Magyar peasants (no better than animals, Gerhard thought), it was an unexpected boon. Stammer shrugged his shoulders and raised his voice: he wanted nothing more to do with Hochbichler-Mengele; the man had to leave right away. Gerhard finally agreed, on the understanding that he first be allowed to get in touch with their benefactor's family in Günzburg – 'a little patience, dear friend' – until which time, he warned, stroking the revolver in his pocket, not a word, no sudden moves. The Nazis in Brazil were powerful, and a denunciation would cost him dear. 'Geza, just think about your children's future . . .'

47.

A few weeks later, Gerhard's Ford Anglia emerged from a cloud of dust and stopped outside the Stammers' farm. The Austrian opened the car door to reveal a squat man, rumpled by a long transatlantic journey and a drive of many kilometres down dirt tracks. 'Mr Hans', the devil's clerk, held a black leather brief-case in his left hand connected to his wrist by a silver chain. He pulled out a sealed envelope. He, too, was thinking of the future of the Stammer boys, Roberto and Miklos, as he caressed their blond heads: here was $2,000 to buy some time and thank their parents, because neither Gerhard nor Rudel had managed to find a new home for their friend Hochbichler. The Stammers had no choice but to wait. Gerhard would get back to them as fast as possible and help them get rid of their cumbersome guest.

Sedlmeier went on a short walk with Mengele before leaving and was shocked. His usually dapper friend was unrecognis-able; he was like a scarecrow with his hollow unshaven cheeks. Since the Stammers had discovered his identity he had been eaten alive by anxiety, traumatised by the news about Eichmann's trial in Jerusalem, which he followed ever more closely whenever he came across a newspaper. He begged Sedlmeier to get him out of this trap. He was exhausted, run ragged by his never-ending flight, hiding out, leading the life of a recluse, of a hunted animal among jaguars and anteaters. He could no longer bear the savannah and this accursed heat. Already he was incapable of reading three pages in a row; soon, he would go completely crazy. Sedlmeier helped him stand up straight and handed him a handkerchief after dusting down his gabardine suit. The Mengeles would not give up on him, and their money could move mountains. Martha, who had just settled in Merano in South Tyrol with Karl-Heinz, was very courageous, a loyal German wife; she had refused to speak to any journalists. She was totally trustworthy. Mengele could not help asking about Irene. In great shape, radiant as ever, Sedlmeier admitted ruefully. Rolf was also doing well in Freiburg, but he snubbed his cousins and the family, as he was under his mother's influence. He was studying law. Sedlmeier stared into Mengele's reddened eyes, and told him they had to stop corresponding, it was too dangerous. Strangers prowled around the factory and the family home in Günzburg. Martha felt watched in Merano. The previous month, two electricians had come to her house without being asked. He must speak only to Gerhard.

The ensuing weeks on the Nova Europa farm were stormy. Hot rain drenched the savannah; the Stammer boys avoided Uncle Peter; Geza worried himself sick at the thought of leaving his family at the mercy of a fanatical Nazi or a possible Mossad raid while he wandered the countryside, far from his family, for meagre wages. Gitta watched Hochbichler's every move. Silent and scowling at the dinner table, he looked away when she tried to catch his eye. As soon as supper was over, he double-locked himself into his room, where Gitta could hear him mumbling and pacing the floor. Hochbichler barked instructions at the workers in the fields of corn, and exploded with rage if they did not show respect, or failed to understand his pidgin Portuguese. At least, noted Gitta, those three slackers (two blacks, one mixed-race) were scared of him and worked hard, whereas they were usually indolent with Geza because he lacked authority. The war criminal had clout.

A month went by without Gerhard showing up. Geza was increasingly tense. He finally announced to his wife that he would take Hochbichler to São Paulo, by force if need be, the following week. The farce had gone on long enough. Gerhard or another fanatic could rescue him, it was none of his business, and if the Nazis harassed them he would spill the beans to a local journalist he knew. His wife was totally against this plan. The doctor was probably armed, and his Austrian friend might pull any kind of sick stunt to protect him. She had a better idea: the Stammers were useful to the Mengeles, those rich Bavarians, who would refuse them nothing. Hochbichler's arrival – she could not bring herself to call him Mengele – was an extra-ordinary stroke of luck. Instead of dumping him in the wild, it was better to up the ante and ask Gerhard for another large lump sum. Or maybe the fugitive's family could buy them a big farm in a less harsh region. After that, they could always find a way to get rid of him; Hochbichler would not live with them forever.

The Stammers quarrelled in the glow of flickering candles. Geza told his wife that she had lost her mind; Gitta retorted that it was all his fault. Had he found a better way to fix their life they would not need to host an insane German to make ends meet. He had promised her the wonders of the world before they married. How much longer would they have to live in this mousetrap? Did he think about the future of their boys? Money was required for their education. And if the police happened to arrest Hochbichler, what were the risks? They could say that they did not know his true identity and that Gerhard had conned them.

Geza finally gave in to his wife's arguments. He passed on their new demands to the Austrian in São Paulo, who acted fast this time. The Mengeles agreed to buy the Stammers a new farm, or rather, they would put up half the capital, and it was up to the Stammers to find this second homestead and sell off their Nova Europa land to pay the rest. The deal was done. A few weeks later, the Stammers and Hochbichler moved to an isolated farmhouse in Serra Negra, surrounded by forty-five hectares. This happened five months before Mossad found little Yossele.

48.

On 1 June 1962, soon after his arrival in Serra Negra, Mengele hears that Eichmann has been hanged in the courtyard of Ramla Prison. He is devastated. As soon as the news is broadcast on Roberto's radio, he dashes off to his room to mull over his fear and despair: that fear which clings to him and which has paralysed and hobbled him ever since he left his cocoon in Buenos Aires.

Eichmann exterminated by the Jews! His ashes scattered in the Mediterranean to stop his wife and sons from visiting his grave! Mengele trembles, his forehead is beaded with cold sweat, he blackens pages and pages of spiral-bound school notebooks with cramped writing, talking about himself in the third person under the name Andreas. He would never have imagined devoting more than three lines to Eichmann, that embittered and odious Austrian, but now, paying tribute to the man who did not denounce him, he is awash with self-pity over his own fate, and prepares his own defence, as self-obsessed as ever. Eichmann, the scapegoat and the outcast, scribbles Mengele. The Germans betrayed him and abandoned him to the vengeful fury of the Jews. One day they will regret sacrificing such men of honour who fought until their last bullet was fired for the homeland and the Führer. Shame on the Germans, what wimps and cowards, a nation of mediocre shopkeepers emasculated by cheapskate leaders, sold to the highest bidders, the merchants from the Temple: they got rid of Eichmann! They shot him in the back! He who did his duty while we just followed orders, in the name of Germany, for Germany, for the greatness of our beloved country.

Those ungrateful Germans are now nailing us to the cross and are allowing themselves to be manipulated by our worst enemies. Which country in the world punishes its most zealous servants and its greatest patriots? Adenauer's Germany is an ogre that devours its children. We will all suffer the same fate, one by one. Poor us . . .

Mengele has never felt quite so alone as on this stormy night. As he pours out his bile and chews at his moustache, lightning zigzags across the night sky and the firmament roars, as if 'Stalin's organs' were pounding the hilltop where Fazenda Santa Lúcia, the new farm, is perched. Hell and damnation, he mumbles, good God how low he has fallen these past three years, wiped off the face of the earth, vanished, insignificant, clinging to life by two fragile threads – the Hungarian family that will betray him sooner or later, and that busybody cryp-to-fascist loser Gerhard. These slender cords might snap at any moment. It's terrifying! At dawn Mengele collapses, sweating, onto his bed.

49.

A crossroads bathed in white light, surrounded by tall buildings without doors or windows, their chimneys reaching up to the sky. The air is thick with the stench of burned flesh. At the centre of this scene stands Josef Mengele. He is twenty years younger, wearing his SS Death's Head uniform. The place is deserted and drenched in blood. Large black birds of prey circle overhead. Mengele's gleaming boots slosh about in the blood as he turns this way and that, helpless, unable to find his bearings.

He discerns eight openings but which one should he choose? A muffled sound comes from the right, like a cascading waterfall, a drum roll, it's getting louder, thundering now, the barking of dogs . . . yes, there's a pack of dogs approaching the junction. Mengele rushes to the left and down an alley, splashing blood all over himself, but the animals are coming closer; he does not see them but he can hear them. Gathering his strength he accelerates, swings left, right, left again, panting. The yelping suddenly stops and the smell of charred meat fades. Mengele can only hear the panicked palpitations of his heart, and a piercing whistle, as he reaches the next crossroads. A cobra rears up to the right and blocks the way to a bust of Hitler. He turns left regretfully and heads down a long corridor lined with thousands of reproductions of the Virgin illuminated by gold candlesticks, each with seven branches. He is cold and thirsty and hungry; he is in blood up to his ankles and yet more blood trickles down the walls. Yet his hope returns when he sees a very bright light at the end of the tunnel, and hears familiar voices and the laughter of women and children. At last he will exit the labyrinth. But no, damn it, he is back at the junction where he started: he's gone full circle. People are celebrating and playing music on the terrace of a building on the square. The first person who sees him alerts all the others, and they lean over the parapet, point at him, mock and boo, throw olive stones, tomatoes and arrows at him and tip out a cauldron of boiling oil, like in the Middle Ages. Mengele raises his fists but nothing comes out of his mouth. He spots Sassen, Rudel and Fritsch, he is sure of it; they are toasting each other on the terrace along with Medea, that vengeful witch, and terrible Saturn is leaning on his scythe, as the black birds of prey overwhelm him. He throws himself on the ground and crawls up to the nearest alley, covered in blood. The sky darkens and he gets up and runs again, breathless, keeps on running straight ahead for an hour, two hours, an eternity, and is back again at the original junction.

Night falls, and a crescent moon illuminates the square, which is calm once more. The blood has gone, as though sucked up by the ochre-coloured earth. Shop windows have appeared on the ground level of the brick buildings. Each one is home to a large black-and-white television set. Mengele goes up to one and sees reflected his aged features and his wide-brimmed hat, his moustache and white gabardine lab coat. On the screen he sees Martha sitting cross-legged on the deck of a ship waving at him. In a second window, the television screen shows a teenage Rolf reading a book and brushing his hand through his hair. He does not raise his eyes to look at his father. In a third window, Mengele watches Irene making love with the shoe merchant from Freiburg. He bangs on the glass as hard as he can, but it is bullet proof, so he flees in agony to the next screen, which is broadcasting a funeral, that of Karl Sr; he can decipher his father's name on a wreath of flowers. He recognises his brother, Alois, with his wife Ruth and his son Dieter in the procession, and Sedlmeier, who is all dressed in black and looks shattered as he offers his wife his arm. Günzburg's town councillors follow.

A bell tolls the Angelus.

Mengele wakes up, burning with fever.

50.

His condition worsens over the following days. Mengele keeps to his bed, delirious and barely eating. Gitta is worried: what if the war criminal dies in her home? Naturally, Geza is not there to help her. As she prepares to go for a doctor, the patient gets his strength back and says to forget the idea. The fever returns on the sixth day. Gitta comes regularly, airs his room, brings him soup and big bowls of tea, and applies cold compresses to his forehead. She now calls him Peter. One humid afternoon when her sons are at school and the workers out in the fields, she slips an impatient hand under the covers, strokes and pulls at the patient's coiled member. Mengele writhes and moans as the Hungarian farm woman rides him, skirt raised high. Then Gitta ties her hair back up and disappears in silence.

She has languished in this torrid wilderness for fifteen years. Always alone, looking after the children, spurning advances from the employees, digging the sterile soil; forever tending the flower beds, trying to economise, cooking, sewing, cleaning while Geza is away God knows where, only returning home one out of three weekends with an empty wallet and a bunch of flowers to make amends for his constant failures. He has stolen her youth. Gitta once dreamed of leading the glittering life of a star ballerina, performing in Budapest or with the Vienna

Opera Ballet. She is convinced that she just had bad luck. In Debrecen, her birthplace, the director of the dance company where she was honing her talents shattered her career by favouring her rival, whom he put onstage in the capital, even though she was far less talented. Jewish bastard, Gitta tells her children, God's punishment was to send him and his family to one of those concentration camps that, a few years later, were all over Eastern Europe. They were never seen again. But for Gitta it was all over: war, exile, marriage and pregnancy, she went through it all. Time had done its destructive work.

At age forty-two, her legs are still firm, her posture unbowed, her buttocks brazen and rounded. Heat and damp and promiscuity: Brazil has caught her fit body unawares. Just a few days after Geza's departure, Gitta is always frustrated. Once, only once before Hochbichler arrived, she succumbed, to a burly mixed-race farmhand who was passing through. It took her months to recover from her feeling of intense shame.

She is attracted to Peter. His greying temples, his moustache and his way of smoothing back his hair remind her of Argentine racing-car drivers in glossy magazines. His eyes are shifty. Gitta appreciates his firm hand, which is indispensable to her now that seven farm workers have been hired to cultivate the rich red soil of the new farm. And she is excited to host a man who is like a character in a spy novel. Finally, a rush of adrenalin . . . Serves you right, Geza, she thinks to herself, I warned you often enough!

She was impressed by the way Peter operated on a cow's abdominal hernia in Nova Europa, a few weeks before their move. He opened up the animal, which was deformed by a huge mass hanging down to the ground, operated on the hernia, and sewed back the skin with artful dexterity. The cow now has an insignificant scar and is in great shape. Thanks to his talents, she can save on costly veterinary fees, and she is delighted. Just the other day, Peter made her laugh. He found an anthill. Rather than set it on fire, he hung a weight from a rope wrapped around a eucalyptus branch. He made calculations and drew for hours like a student engineer, perfecting the height of the pulley to crush the anthill. He was especially busy and enthusiastic after its annihilation, far more than he ever was after they had sex. A few hours later, the termite colony built a nest farther away.

Peter is not memorable in bed, since he has neither Geza's strength nor his imagination. But he is at her beck and call on tedious sultry afternoons. He cannot refuse her; it isn't in his interest to do so. As Gitta expected, the dollars rain down; she just has to complain to Gerhard to get more. She has bought herself two dresses in a shop in Serra Negra, and leather satchels for the boys. A new bed is on its way. And electricity is a blessing.

51.

Startled at first by Gitta's assault, Mengele gathers his wits about him and assesses the situation. He does not like her. That peroxide blonde hair is as vulgar as her manners and her dull eyes; her greasy face still bears traces of acne. Her mouth is intimidating and he guesses that her teeth must be rotten, so foul was her breath when he was bedridden and she kept talking to him. She speaks better German than her idiotic husband, though her Hungarian accent is insufferable. But Gitta is his life insurance. If he keeps her under his thumb, he can go on hiding at the Stammers'. So he lets her have his body. And he likes Fazenda Santa Lúcia. The farm is buried in vegetation, the climate is more temperate than that of Nova Europa, the landscape is gentle, and he is fascinated by all the butterflies, the size of an adult's hand, with red, azure, orange or black-and-white dotted wings. The jungle has supplanted the yellowed savannah. Hills and woods conceal crystalline spring water: Serra Negra is a spa town, founded by Italian settlers. Perched on its hill like a medieval fortress, the farm overlooks the plain. In torment since the hanging of Eichmann, Mengele feels relatively safe here, more than in any of his other hideouts since he left Argentina. Behind the farm and coffee plantation there is a rocky outcrop: a natural wall of wild cliffs and impenetrable forests protect his back.

Mengele never leaves the farm and sees no one other than Gerhard, who brings him newspapers, books, laxative suppositories and, occasionally, classical music records. Before allowing the Stammers to welcome the rare visitors – neighbours, wealthy Germans, Italian colonists – he bombards them with questions: who are they, where do they come from, how long have you known them? Even when reassured, he stays out of sight. Every Saturday, he disappears as soon as he has greeted the friends of Roberto and Miklos who come to play in the afternoon. He is *tio Pedro*, Uncle Peter, the eccentric old Swiss fellow who cannot be photographed or spoken about outside the farm. He asks the Stammers to hire a janitor; his family will pay. He lives surrounded by dogs, a pack of about fifteen strays he has trained, and they accompany him when he goes out into the jungle. The pack leader, Cigano, sticks close to his heels. Central to his defence is a lookout tower six metres high, which he has had built by a farm labourer under the pretext of needing it for bird watching. Because of the risk of termites, the original wooden construction on the site is replaced by a stone edifice: an impressive watchtower now adjoins the farm. Dressed in a beekeeper's outfit, Zeiss binoculars around his neck, Mengele scrutinises the small country road, which winds through the hills, and the purple-hued dirt track leading up to the farm for hours every day. Nothing escapes him. In clear weather he can see far into the distance, as far as the village of Lindonia five miles away. He climbs up his watchtower in a twilight swarming with mosquitoes and scans the darkness. Whether alert, depressed or drowsy, whatever his mood, he listens again and again to Wagner's operas and Bach's cantatas on the Teppaz portable record player bought for him by Gerhard in São Paulo. When he finally goes to bed, his dogs stand guard.

52.

The days, the weeks, the months roll by, and Mengele stagnates in Brazil, in his open-air prison, far from the company of men, a life paralysed by an incessant buzzing, by alternating wet and dry seasons, hurricanes, airless heat, languid rain, surrounded by centipedes, snakes, scorpions and parasitic worms, by euca-lyptus and jackfruit trees, their intertwined roots like monstrous dinosaur feet.

Mengele is often ill. Infected by a bacterium or possibly malaria, he is assailed by migraines, and aches and pains that are accompanied by nausea and diarrhoea, intense chills and high temperatures. He sleeps badly and not enough. He is plagued by nightmares and visions that he can no longer suppress: the flames of crematoria, dying children whose eyes are pinned up on his laboratory walls like butterflies, Eichmann in his glass cage in the Jerusalem courtroom, a rabbi with long red curls who extracts his bones and throws them into bubbling human fat. He hears voices, moaning and weeping, the wailing sirens of Stukas dive-bombing Fazenda Santa Lúcia.

There are moments when he manages to forget the cul-de-sac in which he has ended up, and the fear that gnaws daily at his entrails. His dogs obey his every move and lick him lovingly. He relaxes by doing odd jobs and carpentry, making small objects. He is interested in tropical flowers and botany, as Napoleon was when confined on St Helena. He also writes: bombastic poems and the beginning of an epic narrative, an exhaustive portrayal of his childhood and his formative years, intended for Karl-Heinz and Rolf should he ever manage to get out of this accursed rathole.

Everything else is painful and a struggle. Gitta spies on him, scratches at his door, harasses him constantly. He can refuse nothing to the Madame Bovary of the tropics: at night when the boys are asleep or a quickie in the afternoon behind the mango tree as soon as the labourers' backs are turned. Working in the fields and coffee plantation bores him; the cows and pigs tire him. He is definitely not made for the agrarian utopia of the SS, contact with mother earth, a healthy lifestyle, the great outdoors. So Mengele takes his revenge on the agricultural workers, whom he bullies as if they were serfs and he a Russian landowner. He forbids them to smoke or drink alcohol, even on Sundays: a drunk peasant is dismissed on the spot. He may have despised the Argentines, but he truly hates the Brazilians: half-breeds every one of them, mixing Indian, African and European blood. To a fanatical race theorist who mourns the abolition of slavery, they are the spawn of the Antichrist. He regularly notes down observations in his diary. Miscegenation is a curse, the root cause of cultural decline. Its results can be seen in the workers' perpetual good mood – 'little monkeys', notes Mengele – their nonchalance, their extemporisation and merry muddle, which he finds so intensely irritating. 'Insofar as Brazilians are racial bastards, the heterogeneity of their materiality is characterised by a schizophrenia of the mind. They lack pure conscience and clear will; various contradictory states of being coexist and do battle within them. They are a slippery, disruptive and dangerous race, like the Jews, whereas healthy and decisive minds spring from a biological makeup that stays loyal to its racial identity.'

The reserved Hochbichler is replaced by Mengele the despot, who creeps in everywhere. Better school attendance is expected from Roberto and Miklos, along with better school marks and discipline, as he would demand of his own sons. Their German is abysmal and he rarely misses an opportunity to point this out. They'd do better to study music than hang out with village troublemakers and hunt bats with catapults. He forbids them to chew gum in his presence and advises them to be wary of girls and to associate only with the sons of Europeans. He is dead set against the surprise party Roberto is planning for his fifteenth birthday. The day he caught them listening to a Beatles single on his portable record player in the watchtower, he exploded with rage. Never had the Stammer boys endured such a verbal drubbing – Gitta had to intervene. He is also at odds with her. Mengele takes great pleasure in sniping at her. She sleeps too long and should be more careful about what she eats, brush her teeth more fastidiously, not smoke so much. He criticises her for dressing frumpily like a peasant girl and for scratching her arse in front of the labourers. Her cooking is bad; she uses too much salt and paprika; she needs to concentrate, choose ingredients for her sauces and purées that produce a more subtle flavour. Her housecleaning could be improved.

Obsessively tidy, Mengele has a pathological horror of dirt. Woe betide the person who disturbs his rigid, orderly lifestyle by borrowing his pen, his scissors, or a book, or moving a chair or rug. He flies into a dark rage, yelling and moaning, as if the disappearance of an object has shaken the fragile foundations of his existence, illuminating the nothingness of his immense solitude.

53.

In the middle of that year, 1963, Mengele finally receives news of his family. Through the good offices of Gerhard the postman, who gets news from Sedlmeier, he finds out that the investigators have deserted Günzburg and Martha is no longer being tailed in Merano. His pursuers seem to have put their campaign on hold once again.

Following the time-consuming but successful Operation Tiger, the Mossad unit has refocused on the Middle East. Its director, Harel, is under extreme pressure to deal with a very serious threat. Israel is in danger of being annihilated. In July 1962, Egypt tested a ballistic missile capable of reaching anywhere in its territory. At a triumphal military parade through the streets of Cairo, President Gamal Abdel Nasser displayed his new rockets, which can be shot 600 kilometres. Nazi scientists and technicians, veterans of Hitler's V2 programme, advise the Egyptian guided-missile experts. Nine hundred rockets are under construction on an ultra-secret site, Factory 333; the most alarmist reports warn that they are designed to carry radioactive waste or nuclear warheads.

Mossad is failing in its core mission of assuring Israel's security, squandering its meagre resources Nazi-hunting in South America and tracking down little Yossele. These sensational stories have made Harel world famous, but the Mossad boss is jeered. His detractors criticise him for turning the agency into a public relations office. To prove them wrong, Harel launches Operation Damocles: a covert campaign of violence against the German scientists involved in the Egyptian rocket programme. Some receive letter bombs, others are kidnapped or murdered. When Israeli agents threaten the daughter of a West German electronic guidance expert, they are arrested in Switzerland and charged with coercion and attempted murder; a public scandal breaks out, jeopardising relations between Federal Germany and the Jewish state and its economic and military interests. Harel is forced to resign and is replaced by Gen. Meir Amit. Tracking down Nazis is not his priority. Mossad must focus on gathering information and waging the fight against Israel's Arab enemies. Israel needs allies, and the kidnapping of Eichmann was not well received by the international community. States do not play games with one another's sovereignty.

Israel gears up for the decisive Six-Day War. Mengele's capture is relegated to the background.

54.

Early in 1964, Mengele receives some terrible news. As he reads Martha's letter, he feels as though a dagger has pierced his ribs, the blade buried deep in his heart: he has been stripped of his diplomas. Because he violated the Hippocratic oath and committed murders in Auschwitz, the universities of Frankfurt and Munich have withdrawn his doctoral degrees in medicine and anthropology.

All that effort, all those sacrifices reduced to nothing by some obscure bureaucrats . . . Mengele is devastated. To think that he, the surgeon of the people, the recipient of numerous awards, the great hope of genetic research, should be robbed of his treasured qualifications, the source of his greatest pride, and his experiments discredited as if he were some vulgar charlatan!

Mengele burns his wife's letter, leaves the plantation and heads into the jungle to wallow in his disgrace, flanked by his dogs. Accursed, unjust Germany, for whose sake he has done his duty as a foot soldier of Nazi bio-politics. A generation ago, the Germans considered Darwinism and eugenics to be the foundations of a modern functional society. Everybody wanted to study biology because it paved the way to a prestigious and rewarding career. Yes, mutters Mengele to his mongrel Cigano,

German society reasoned purely in biological terms. Race and bloodlines were the fundamentals of life, law, war, sex, international relations and the supreme science of medicine. At university, his entire class admired ancient Greece, where the evanescent individual bowed to the demands of community and state.

For his generation, the inferior, the unproductive and the parasitic were not fit to live. Hitler guided all of them; Mengele was not alone in following him. Every German was bewitched by the Führer, by the grisly and titanic mission that he had entrusted to them: to heal the people, purify the race, build a social order conforming to nature, acquire Lebensraum and perfect the human species. He had been up to the task, he knew it. How could they blame him? And strip him so easily of his precious degrees? He had been courageous in eliminating disease by eliminating the sick, which was encouraged by the system, permitted by the rule of law: such killing was a state enterprise.

Mad with rage, Mengele gives a flying kick to a termite mound rising up in front of his drooling, barking dogs. German conglomerates filled their pockets in Auschwitz by working the docile labour at their disposal to the point of exhaustion and collapse. Auschwitz was a lucrative venture: before he arrived at the camp, the inmates were already producing synthetic rubber for IG Farben and arms for Krupp. The felt-making factory Alex Zink bought women's hair by the sackload from the Kommandantur and made socks for submarine crews and tubing for railroads. Schering Laboratories paid one of his colleagues to carry out experiments in *in vitro* fertilisation, and Bayer was testing new typhus drugs on camp inmates. Twenty years later, Mengele rants, the leaders of these companies are turncoats. They smoke cigars surrounded by their families, they sip vintage wines in their villas in Munich or Frankfurt, while he is mired in cow shit . . . Traitors! Cowards! Scum! Those industrialists, bankers and politicians worked hand in hand with him at Auschwitz and reaped huge profits in the process, while he, who has not made a pfennig, is left to pick up the bill.

55.

Mengele is bitter that day. As ever, he wallows in self-pity, feeling no remorse or regret, and vents his anger on his four-legged companions and the baobabs of the virgin forest, which whispers and sings to itself, paying him no heed. He sits on a tree trunk in a clearing, head in hands, and remembers his Auschwitz colleagues: twenty SS doctors assigned to work in the camp. Horst Schumann sterilised his subjects by irradiating them with X-rays before castrating the men and removing the women's ovaries. Carl Clauberg implanted the fetuses of animals in the bellies of his human guinea pigs and sterilised them by injecting their uteruses with formaldehyde. The pharmacist Victor Capesius stole the gold dental fillings of still-bleeding corpses to sell outside the camp. Friedrich

Entress inoculated prisoners with typhus and dispatched them by a lethal shot of phenol to the heart. August Hirt injected homosexuals with hormones and murdered deportees in order to perform autopsies that would determine the causes of their racial inferiority, and to pursue anatomical research on the Jewish skeleton. And what of the 350 others who passed through the camps (university professors, biologists, physicians), participating in the T4 Euthanasia Programme, what has become of them? A few committed suicide or were sentenced after the war at the Nuremberg trials, but most have slipped through the cracks and been reintegrated into their families and civil society and resumed their careers. Mengele knows this and it sickens him.

Back at the farm, he climbs up to the top of his watchtower. He weeps, thinking of how brilliantly his mentors, Eugen Fischer and Baron Otmar von Verschuer, have extricated themselves from their pasts. Fischer, the celebrated theorist of eugenics and an inspiration to Hitler, took part in the Herero and Namaqua Genocide in Namibia before retiring to the peaceful town of Freiburg-im-Breisgau, where his lifelong friend the philosopher Martin Heidegger lives in his country retreat. An honorary member of the German Anthropological Society, Fischer has successfully published his memoirs, *Encounters with the Dead*. Mengele's father sent Josef a copy shortly before dying. Von Verschuer, the former director of the Kaiser Wilhelm Institute for Anthropology, Human Heredity and Eugenics in Berlin, to whom Mengele sent marrow, eyes, blood, organs and the skeletons of Auschwitz children, von

Verschuer, a great admirer of the Führer – 'the first statesman to take into account biological inheritance and racial hygiene' – was appointed Professor of Human Genetics at the University of Münster, of which he later became the dean, and he now runs the largest genetic research centre in West Germany. Mengele remembers how once when he was on leave from the Russian front, they went to the cinema together to see *Der ewige Jude*. In the crowded auditorium, they booed with all the other spectators every time the devilish Jew appeared on screen, and crunched raspberry-flavoured boiled sweets decorated with swastikas. The two doctors shared the same passion for Nazism. Mengele wrote to him several times from Argentina, but the baron – who had destroyed their correspondence and incriminating archives at the end of the war – never answered. Neither he nor Fischer was prosecuted.

The son of a bitch, the son of a bitch, whimpers Mengele in his tower, fists clenched.

Fischer died in his bed at the age of ninety-three in 1967; von Verschuer in a car accident two years later.

56.

Geza Stammer hates Mengele. Does he suspect his wife of lying and cheating on him? Of having a tempestuous affair with the cantankerous Nazi? Geza is a carefree, lazy sybarite who likes to drink, smoke and sing. He enjoys his life, which Dr Hochbichler – as he likes to call him to annoy him – does his best to poison whenever Geza returns home to the farm. Mengele despises the Hungarian and does not hide it. Had the Stammer family relied solely on Geza to survive, it would still be languishing in the bush. Thanks to Mengele's money, the family has been able to move and buy agricultural machines that help boost their income; Gitta has been given clothing, bedding and tableware that once she only dreamed of. And she belongs to him. Mengele considers it his right to give advice to the incompetent Geza. He should ask his boss, who exploits him shamelessly, for a pay rise; he and his wife should be stricter with their sons, whose education leaves much to be desired; and Roberto, whose haircut is indecent, would do well to go to the barber more often. Their home is bedlam because the absentee head of the family has no authority. When Geza smokes or drinks a glass of slivovitz, Mengele lectures him, reminding him of the Nazis' battle against cancer, their preventive campaigns against tobacco and chemical additives, their banning of smoking in public places, their introduction of the first non-smoking carriages in the Third Reich's trains. He stops the Stammers from speaking Hungarian at the dinner table, as he is convinced that they are plotting and mocking him. He demands wholemeal bread, which aids his digest-ion, and complains about the Magyar delicacies so loved by Geza and the boys – fish soup with tomatoes and peppers, veal chops stuffed with goose liver. Liszt aside, Mengele despises the Hungarian race, a 'minor people' with a 'subculture'. Geza embodies the flaws of his species, and Mengele likes to point these out when the cuckolded surveyor spends the weekend with his family. The disgraced Bavarian doctor dishes out long historical lectures over lunch about the moral bankruptcy of Hungary, which is inferior in all respects to 'honest and hard-working' Germany. An ambivalent ally during the war, Hungary despoiled two-thirds of its own territory and was duly occupied by the Soviets, 'a fair punishment for a nation of Gypsies which can only produce paprika and salami'.

Although he is on the ropes, Geza manages to dodge Mengele. Cowed in front of his wife and children, he does not counter-punch head-on, since the authoritarian German is too practiced a brawler, but he loves to provoke him with humour and trickery, mocking his theories of race and Teutonic superiority – 'Germany is occupied, too, remember, dear Dr Hochbichler?' – and ridi-culing the Führer, whom he calls an 'impotent vegetarian' and mimics to entertain his wife and children, with a colander on his head, fists clenched, his face in a grimace, spittle foaming at the corners of his mouth. Geza wins every round against Mengele, who continues to venerate Hitler as 'the man of the century, a giant of History, and the heir apparent to Alexander the Great and Napoleon'. Mengele rears up furiously, slams the dining-room door, takes refuge in his watchtower.

Encouraged by his sons and workers, who regularly complain about Hochbichler, Geza has become something of a genius at tormenting the Nazi. One Sunday, he tries to take a photo of him with his new Nikon; the next, he remarks that he spotted a suspicious-looking group of Israeli tourists in the village; on yet another, he teases him for looking like Groucho Marx with his huge moustache. He regularly brings home newspapers reporting Mengele's crimes, the arrest of a Nazi, a trial of war criminals in West Germany, or one of Simon Wiesenthal's victories. Gitta acts as the buffer between the two men most of the time, and can generally calm them down after a flare-up. Otherwise, Gerhard is called and comes to the rescue, bringing peace to the household along with a box of chocolates and a wad of dollars. Then Geza is off on the road again, and Mengele can take back his malevolent hold on the farm.

But on that Easter Monday 1964, a few weeks after Mengele is stripped of his university degrees, the two men come to real blows. On the radio, there is a report about the Auschwitz trials, which have been taking place in Frankfurt over the past few months. Mengele's name is regularly mentioned, with survivors testifying to his crimes and his cruelty. Geza crows: 'You, too, Dr Hochbichler, should be courageous enough to face justice! You have nothing to fear! You only did your duty, didn't you? So why should you feel guilty? Act like a soldier and go back to Germany, so you can tell your compatriots how you fought in Auschwitz against their degeneration, for the health of their race . . .'

One of the innumerable rules Mengele has imposed on the Stammers is strictly non-negotiable: no talk of Auschwitz. Just to speak the name of the camp is taboo. So Mengele goes for Geza's throat, ready to strangle him, and squeezes with all his might. The Hungarian yells and struggles. Gitta and the boys rush to separate them. Miklos pulls the Nazi's hair, Gitta kicks him in the shins and Roberto runs in from the garden waving a rake. Mengele finally relaxes his stranglehold. Geza is scarlet, staggering, screaming, 'He's gone too far this time! It's the end! Get out, Hochbichler, you vermin, get the hell out; fuck off, or I'll call the cops!' A nasty smile plays across Mengele's lips as he stares at the Stammers with deathly disdain. He is burning to spill the beans, to tell Geza his wife is a slut, and to tell his sons that their mother is a degenerate whore, but he holds his fire and chews at his moustache. He managed to escape the clutches of the Red Army during the war, and then the Americans and Mossad, so he's not going to risk his skin for these fuckers. There are four of them, not to mention the workers, who hate his guts and would very likely lend a hand. Mengele calmly crosses his arms over his chest: he is at home here, half the farm is his, so if he packs and leaves, they do, too. Gerhard is summoned fast to sort out the terms of an 'amicable' divorce. Even Gitta gives in at this point: her mental health and the survival of her family are all-important, and Peter has gone too far.

With Sedlmeier's consent and Rudel's help, Gerhard tries to come up with a back-up plan. He discusses an Arab solution with the Stammers: a possible transfer to Egypt, Syria or Morocco, but nothing comes of it, as the whole process is too complicated. No one wants Hochbichler, a leaden weight; his reputation in Nazi circles has travelled across the oceans. His family's pocketbook must take a big hit so that the Stammers will agree to go on hosting this black sheep, this permanent pariah. An arrest would tarnish the legendary reputation, reliability and robustness of the Mengele family firm, which is expanding in Germany and throughout the world. They offer to buy Geza a new car. The Hungarian hems and haws, refuses their offer, and in the end is rewarded with a luxury saloon, his own chauffeur, and an envelope stuffed with cash 'essential for its maintenance', as he puts it to Gerhard.

And the odious threesome carry on as before.

57.

In February 1965, Herberts Cukurs's corpse is found in a crate in Montevideo. Nicknamed 'the hangman of Riga' and 'the Latvian Eichmann', the famous aviator used to set fire to synagogues filled with Jews and burn them alive. He was shot dead by an avenging commando unit of Mossad calling itself 'those who will never forget'. His executioners pinned their typed verdict to his corpse: *'Given the seriousness of the crimes of which Herberts Cukurs is accused, particularly his personal responsibility for the assassination of 30,000 men, women and children, and given the monstrous cruelty shown by Herbert Cukurs during the execution of his crimes, we condemn the said Cukurs to death.'*

When Mengele finds out about this friend's death, he becomes doubly vigilant. He surrounds himself with more dogs, buys more powerful binoculars and spends longer hours scrutinising the surrounding countryside from his watchtower. One night, from his eyrie he spots two beams of light. The headlights flash on and off as they approach. Mengele's heart is in his mouth. A vehicle climbs the hill, his dogs growl, and he loads his gun, takes aim, trembling, at the darkness. He wants to climb down from his lookout post, but his legs will not support him. The car stops in front of the gate. He hears slamming doors and the voices of young men, muttering, and can just make out stealthy shadows. His dogs bark, and it makes him jump when suddenly a voice yells, 'It's me, it's me!' Roberto has been out partying with friends.

Mengele also strengthens the security around his written correspondence with Germany, using only initials; it is child's play. He is 'P', Rolf is 'R', In situ One, Serra Negra . . . His sealed letters are addressed to a P.O. box in Switzerland or, more rarely, to a family friend in Augsburg; Sedlmeier then retrieves them and dispatches them. His mail is delivered to a P.O. box in Brazil in Gerhard's name. Mengele's spidery writing is easily identifiable, so he begins to use a typewriter.

In the middle of 1964, a few months before Cukurs's execution, he had narrowly escaped some serious trouble: His method of communicating with Günzburg was almost rumbled. In Frankfurt, Bauer, the prosecutor, issued a search warrant for Sedlmeier's home, convinced he was the go-between for Mengele and his family. But the police found no letters, and not a trace of any compromising evidence. He had been warned in the nick of time that a raid was imminent, thanks to a call from his police contact.

Since serving warrants for Mengele's arrest, the West German judicial authorities have been tracking him without much conviction. It took them over a year to send fingerprints to their embassies in South America. When Mengele was still a travelling salesman in Paraguay, he met a typist from the embassy in the German colony. She had sprained her ankle and he treated her. She knew his name but not his past. Back in Asunción, the young woman was surprised to find that the doctor was not registered with the consulate, and she reported it to the diplomatic service. An assiduous investigation was carried out leading the chargé d'affaires to Krug, whose lies were taken at face value.

Bonn devotes no special resources to tracking down Mengele, sending neither agents nor spies. Its intelligence agencies are infested with former Nazis who could easily approach Rudel, Sassen, Krug or von Eckstein, none of whom have ever made a secret of their loyalty to the Third Reich. The German Federal Republic is a stickler for procedure and just puts a reward on the doctor's head for crimes against humanity. When its diplomatic services get hold of copies of documents attesting that Mengele has been given Paraguayan citizenship, the hunt focuses on that country. The West Germans are convinced that Mengele lives in Asunción or in the region of Alto Paraná. In 1962, they request his extradition. Gen. Stroessner, who has been informed by Rudel of Mengele's departure to Brazil, refuses to cooperate. He derives great pleasure from muddying the tracks: Mengele may have left the country, but if he is arrested on his territory, Stroessner will refuse to extradite him. Paraguay defends its citizens. The following year, Chancellor Adenauer pledges a bounty of 10 million US dollars in aid if Paraguay delivers the doctor. The dictator will not hear of it. Bonn concludes that the highest authorities in Paraguay are protecting the fugitive.

In 1964, while the world's eyes are on the Auschwitz trials in Frankfurt, the West Germans increase the pressure. The Ministry of Foreign Affairs makes a public announcement that Mengele is now a Paraguayan citizen who resides in the tri-border area and often travels to Brazil. The German ambassador in Asunción asks Stroessner to strip Mengele of his citizenship on the grounds that he lied to obtain it. The president reiterates that Mengele is long gone and West German interference is totally unacceptable: if His Excellency continues in this vein, he will be persona non grata; a foreign power cannot under-mine the sovereignty of Paraguay. A few months later, in tandem with the raid on Sedlmeier's home, Fritz Bauer holds a press conference: a reward of 50,000 marks will be paid to whomever captures Mengele. The Nazi doctor is currently living in freedom under his true identity in Paraguay; he has a lot of money and is protected by friends in high places. The Paraguayan interior minister refutes the prosecutor's claims, stating that Mengele is hiding in Brazil or Peru. No one believes in the Stroessner government's denials when, the following year, a former SS officer is arrested in Paraguay and swears he has bumped into the doctor on several occasions.

The West Germans have hit a wall. In 1965 they appoint a new ambassador to Asunción. His brief is to improve relations between the two states. There are many first- and second-generation

Germans in Paraguay, and the country is an important pawn in Western global policy, which aims to block the Marxist guerrilla movements that Moscow and Havana operate remotely in South America. The Federal Republic of Germany eases the pressure in the hunt for Mengele.

The Israelis no longer track him; the Syro-Egyptian threat is now clear and their survival is at stake. That Mossad did not pass on the Brazilian information to the German intelligence agencies is understandable, but why not contact Bauer directly, as he was the one who delivered Eichmann?

It is a mystery.

58.

With governments constrained by the contingencies of realpolitik, the void is filled by journalists and Nazi hunters drawn by the lure of glory, the scoop of a lifetime or money. They, too, scour Paraguay, building the legend of a supervillain as elusive as Goldfinger, a pop-culture figure of evil incarnate: invincible, wealthy, cunning, capable of shaking off his pursuers and escaping from the most perilous situations completely unscathed. In the 1960s James Bond is a box-office icon, while Dr Mengele becomes a brand, his name alone enough to freeze your blood and to boost sales of books and magazines. He is the archetypal cold, sadistic Nazi: a monster.

We see Mengele in a T-shirt filmed for a few seconds by a Brazilian for a Czech documentary. The man allegedly calls himself Dr Engwald, lives on the border of Paraguay and Argentina, and sails a boat named the *Viking* on the Paraná river. Mengele is an irresistible seducer: an Argentine journalist discovers that he has gone to ground in a farm near the Paraguayan city of Altos, a gorgeous woman in tow. Despite his age he is in good shape, likes to dance and enjoys social events. A former SS officer believes Mengele has had cosmetic surgery, like his friend Martin Bormann, who did not die in Berlin in 1945, but dines regularly with Mengele in the best restaurants of Asunción and La Paz. A boatman confesses that a taciturn, misunderstood Mengele – who has a beard – regularly crosses the Paraná. One of Bormann's former bodyguards reveals to the *Sunday Times* that Mengele has joined the logistical command of the Paraguayan army in the north of the country, where he officiates as a doctor. In May 1966, the Brazilian police mediate the capture of 'Mengele', who on closer examination turns out to be a German tourist. Two years later, an old cop swears he shot him on board a boat sailing down the Paraná. Hit in the chest and neck, the Angel of Death fell into the water and drowned.

The myth of the elusive murderer owes a lot to Simon Wiesenthal. The family of the former deportee came from Galicia and was exterminated during the Holocaust. Weisenthal, its lone survivor, started to gather information about Nazi war criminals after the war, in Linz and then in Vienna, where he founded the Jewish Documentation Centre.

He became an international star after the publication of his autobiography, *I Hunted Eichmann*, in which he claimed he took a more decisive role in the capture of the SS officer than he actually did; Bauer's groundwork remains a secret and Mossad's agents are bound by the strictest confidentiality. In the eyes of the general public, particularly in America, this crafty, charming man, who wears tweed jackets and speaks English and German with a Yiddish accent, is the personification of the solitary vigilante. He regularly receives death threats at his Viennese office – on the wall of which hangs a daunting map of every Nazi concentration camp. He is the last Mohican of the vanished world of Central and Eastern European Jewry. He may have been involved in uncovering numerous prominent Nazi war criminals, and he tirelessly campaigned to ensure that West Germany did not impose a statute of limitations on the fugitives but he is, above all else, a phenomenal storyteller, one who demonstrated an early mastery of the media. Now that Eichmann has been tried and executed, he devotes much of his inexhaustible energy to tracking down Mengele. With his network failing him, and with little real knowledge about where the doctor might have gone to ground, Wiesenthal keeps the world's interest stoked by embroidering unlikely stories. No one must forget the evil doings of the white-gloved doctor of Auschwitz; he must not be allowed to feel safe anywhere.

In July 1967, Wiesenthal publishes *The Murderers Among Us*. He dedicates a chapter to Mengele, entitled 'The Man Who Collected Blue Eyes'.

He appropriates the story of a Mossad agent who was murdered in the mountain town of Bariloche and takes pains to elaborate upon some compelling details: the attractive blonde spy – naturally – had been sterilised at Auschwitz by Mengele, who later recognised her in Bariloche, identifying the tattoo on her forearm while they danced. He then forced her over a precipice as she was hiking down a mountain footpath.

Mengele is portrayed as a ubiquitous jet-setter, who Wiesenthal hunts in Peru, Chile, Brazil and the most remote Paraguayan army camps. Surrounded by bodyguards, he frequents the finest restaurants in Asunción and drives a powerful black Mercedes. After Nasser denies him entry into Egypt, he sets sail on a yacht with Martha to the Greek island of Kythnos. Alerted, Wiesenthal sends a journalist to entrap the fugitives. The manager of the Unique Hotel in the Cyclades islands confirms that a German and his wife left the establishment the day before and boarded a sailing boat to an unknown destination. 'Mengele won that round,' writes Wiesenthal; he wins the next one too, when he escapes a commando raid by a group of Auschwitz survivors, the 'Committee of Twelve', who arrive to kidnap him at the Hotel Tirol in the Paraguayan city of Encarnación one 'dark, hot night' in March 1964. Mengele is a man with a sixth sense, a magician. 'It's one o'clock in the morning when men charge up the stairs and smash down the door of room number twenty-six on the second floor. It is empty, the bedding still warm. Alerted by telephone of the imminent arrival of these avengers, Mengele fled into the jungle in pyjamas ten minutes ago.'

Wiesenthal withholds one major revelation from readers until the book's end: the exact location of the war criminal in 1967. 'Mengele lives . . . in the military zone between Puerto San Vincente, on the Asunción–São Paulo highway, and Fortress Carlos Antonio López, located at the border, on the Paraná river. He lives in a small white hut, in an area of the jungle landscaped by German immigrants. Only two roads lead to his secluded home; both roads are patrolled by soldiers and the Paraguayan police, who are ordered to stop all cars and shoot anyone who disregards orders. In the event of the police making a mistake, four bodyguards, armed to the teeth and equipped with radios and walkie-talkies, keep watch over Mengele. He pays for them out of his own pocket.'

59.

In September 1967, while the world envisions fantastic stories about his evil omnipotence, Mengele frets alone in bed in his lair in Serra Negra, which he has not left since arriving five years previously. He is gripped by anxiety yet again. He should not have read that old copy of *Der Spiegel* that Gerhard found in a petrol station. He is irritated by an interview given by Albert Speer on his recent release from Spandau prison in Berlin, after twenty years of incarceration. Mengele choked reading of the contrition of Hitler's architect, a 'criminal' in his eyes. So, he was ignorant of the extermination of the Jews? Him, the Führer's favourite, Reich minister of armaments and war production, who made good use of the concentration camps for forced labour? Mengele tosses aside the magazine, enraged at the sight of Speer posing sheepishly in front of his grand Heidelberg villa. He will not get back to sleep now, so up he gets and off he goes to his watchtower.

Deep in darkness, he listens to a Schumann violin concerto, offset by the steady buzzing background noise of the tropics that fizzes day and night. The wind waltzes over the leaves, and the noxious smell of rotten jackfruit drifting in from outside accompanies Mengele's ruminations on Schumann's untimely death, his musical hallucinations, and on Bernhard Förster's suicide in a hotel room after the failure of Nueva Germania – which he had founded with his wife, Elisabeth Nietzsche. On time passing: the immutable cycle of the seasons, reflected in the landscape, exacerbates his unease at being in a country that wears him down so. He misses the autumn mists, the first snows of November, the meadows dotted with flowers in the spring, and the silvery lakes of his distant youth. Mengele knows that no one escapes from an open prison. He wonders if he should not put an end to his days rather than endure the vacuity and torture of exile, abandon this game of Snakes and Ladders that he is destined to lose as his allies betray him and his enemies proliferate.

Franz Stangl, former commandant of the Sobibor and Treblinka extermination camps, was arrested back in February at his home in São Paulo by the Brazilian authorities and swiftly extradited to the German Federal Republic. When the news of his capture was made public, Gerhard indignantly raced to Serra Negra to announce to Mengele that he was considering vouching for the SS officer, his compatriot – 'an exemplary man, one of the best camp commanders in Poland', as he put it, speaking of the man responsible for the mass murder of a million people. Mengele managed to get him to calm down and to curb his neo-Nazi activities in the São Paulo area, which risked attracting the attention of the police and leading them straight to him. To the torments caused by the arrest of Stangl was added the disappointment of the Six Day War, in June, which Mengele followed daily on the television Geza had given his sons some weeks earlier. Nasser is treacherous, no better than Perón. His armies and those of his Arab allies were crushed by those little jewboys, who grabbed Jerusalem, the Golan Heights, Sinai, all of Palestine. Mengele cannot believe it.

Helpless and shivering with cold in his ridiculous watch-tower, he gazes at the blood moon camouflaged by inky rainclouds. That night in September 1967, Mengele senses that he has lost. He understands nothing of the world now – this world to which he no longer belongs, this world that reviles him as 'the devil's servant'. All through the austral winter, he watches young Germans on television challenging the ances-tral order – discipline, hierarchy, authority – and demanding that their fathers explain themselves; he sees long-haired hippies dancing through the streets of San Francisco and making pilgrimages to Kathmandu; he stares in disbelief as white people defend blacks in America. He is disgusted by

155

contemporary German artists and the first communes in Cologne, Munich and West Berlin; by Beuys and his social sculptures moulded from coal, rubble and rusted steel; by the Zero Group; by Richter and Kieffer; by the Viennese Actionism of Brus, Muehl and Nitsch, who lacerate their skin and smear blood on their canvases; and by psychedelic musicians who bury Wagnerian lyricism under wild waves of synthesisers, flutes and percussion. Their cosmic dirges plumb the depths of the German soul and vent their despair by trampling the past. Haunted by the war, sculptors, painters and musicians flee the Germany of slogans and euphemisms, of hypocrisy and lies, the despicable Germany that belonged to their predatory parents, the Germany of iconoclastic fury, the torture chamber, the quagmire of human sins, the Germany they associate with the right-hand panel of Bosch's triptych *The Garden of Earthly Delights*, with Hell and Satan, the source of the great plague that has just ravaged Europe, its factories of death, Auschwitz, Treblinka: Mengele.

60.

Spending the evening in front of the television becomes a ritual for the Stammer family. Mengele digests the news in his slippers, wrapped up in a blanket with Cigano snoozing on his knees. He forces Gitta and the boys to watch the news, to listen to him praise the 'virile' military dictators that rule Brazil and the 'decisive' intervention of the Soviets in Prague, rejoice at the American quagmire in Vietnam, lament the decline of the West caused by 'the gangrene of materialism and individualism and all the garbage imported from the United States since the end of the war' and mock the student uprisings of 1968: 'stateless young fools who confuse anarchy with freedom'. He is angered by news from Germany, by the grand coalition led by 'that Nazi Kiesinger and the deserter Brandt', by 'the weakness and negligence of the leaders'. The Stammer boys chuckle when Uncle Peter curses the ministers – the Nazis who have converted to democracy and appear on the screen – and calls them 'traitors, rats, separatists, liars and arseholes'. He leaps from the sofa and paces up and down the living room swearing his hatred for the Old Testament and for Christianity, 'responsible for the decadence' of his faraway homeland. Sedlmeier, however, has encouraging news: his most dangerous antagonist, the prosecutor Bauer, died under mysterious circumstances on 1 July 1968.

His relationship with Geza remains appalling. The two men bait one another and trade insults. The Hungarian has since made up with his wife, to allay her suspicions of a mistress in São Paulo. To revenge this reversion, Mengele makes a great show of sleeping with farm employees. Gitta moans in Geza's arms and strokes his neck in front of Peter. Gerhard frequently intervenes to calm everyone down. But he is overwhelmed by events in October 1968. The Stammers plan to sell the farm and move, giving up on agriculture altogether. Geza has been promoted and wants to be nearer his workplace. Dr Hochbichler refuses point-blank to abandon his fort. Panicked, the Mengele family contact Rudel, their representative in Paraguay since the catastrophic departure of the family pariah.

A few weeks later, the former air force ace sends some promising news Gerhard's way: Klaus Barbie is prepared to host Mengele. The 'butcher of Lyon' is prospering in Bolivia, having supplied information to United States military counter-intelligence on Communist activities in the army and the French Occupation Zone in Germany. Twice sentenced to death in absentia by military tribunals in Lyon, he now operates under the name of Klaus Altmann in La-Paz. He once ran a company in cahoots with Rudel – ostensibly a logging firm, but with a sideline in narcotics and arms. Now, with the blessing of the CIA and German services, the former Gestapo chief works as a security consultant, training Bolivian officers in harsh interrogation techniques – the military of that country having taken power in 1964.

The juvenile in Gerhard is drawn to the Bolivian option. He pictures himself crossing jungles and borders, a flat houndstooth cap on his head and the dear doctor at his side, on their way to meet Barbie, a man with quite a service record. Mengele will not hear of it. Just the idea of getting into the Austrian's small car makes him freeze in terror. Now that he is nearly sixty, changing country for the umpteenth time is out of the question. He does not know Barbie, but he is certain he would not be able to manipulate him the way he can the Stammers. He is the master of all he sees at Serra Negra: man and beast. He will not take any risks. Besides, Rudel is untrustworthy and has proved to be a disappointment; he has not visited Mengele since he moved to Brazil and forgot his last birthday. Rudel's interest in Mengele lies in the generous commissions he receives on the sale of the family firm's equipment in Paraguay, down to the last wheelbarrow. As for his damn motto, 'He who abandons himself is lost', on that point, at least, he has been true to his word. Rudel, in his cashmere jacket, can take his Bolivian plan and go to hell.

The decision is passed on; Barbie is upset, Rudel furious. 'Mengele is a pain in the arse,' he says to Gerhard. 'He can go it alone from now on. I don't want to hear his name.' Mengele refuses to leave but will not live alone, and the Stammers need his share from the sale of Serra Negra to acquire the property of their dreams: an imposing building on a forested hill. It has four bedrooms, comes with more than 8,000 square metres of land and is about thirty kilometres from São Paulo in the municipality of Caieiras.

Mengele has to force himself to follow them, and so the Stammers to take him along. They move in early 1969.

61.

No watchtower this time, just a fence. Mengele immediately gets to work building fortifications. He drives stakes into the ground, connects them with string, and digs deep holes into which he inserts posts two metres high. The earth is unyielding, so he has to go at it with a pick and an auger. Geza watches, smirking, as the backbreaking work carries on over weeks. Mengele drills his holes, then starts over, set square in hand, because the posts stand crooked on the sloping ground. Then he anchors them with gravel, cement and water; fixes the support beams and finally the vertical planks. Then the three layers of rot-resistant wood are lacquered and painted white. A screen of shrubs and lemon trees is planted behind the palisade. Job done.

Mengele is at a loose end and does not adapt well to his new environment. He had to abandon several of his stray dogs and can only go for walks at dawn and dusk, as the area is more densely populated than the countryside around Serra Negra. He tinkers, repairs the doors and floors, builds bookshelves and avoids the Stammers. Geza is only away for two or three days a week. Mengele would willingly take back Gitta, but she does not want him anymore, disgusted as she is by his volatile mood swings. Mengele often dines alone in the kitchen, or in front of the television. He blackens the pages of his diary, writing tearful poems. He continues his study of wildlife and flora. Mengele spies on banana spiders and beetles, and develops a passion for Blattidae – called cockroaches by the Stammers and everyone else. It is impossible to catch them with bare hands – the beasties can change direction twenty-five times a second, he reads – he lures them with a lump of sugar, or meat, onto the bathroom floor so he can assess the white blood dripping from their injured thoraxes and sketch their large compound eyes in his notebooks; the exoskeleton is brightly coloured and often has psychedelic patterns. A leg grows back as soon as it is ripped off. They have six legs with eighteen joints apiece; their long antennae and the hair-covered segments on their bodies allow them to feel the air and the presence of a predator. Mengele envies these joyful insects for their ignorance of the legal process and the penal code and for their alleged resistance to an atomic bomb. He is delighted to discover·that the German cockroach is the most harmful of its kind: a carrier of germs, it causes allergies in humans. Applied to a wound, powdered cockroach soothes the pain. The next time Gitta cuts herself while preparing a salad, he will apply cockroach balm to the damaged finger; or else to Roberto the hothead's ankle, since he regularly injures himself playing football. The idea amuses him, another quirk of fucking life!

Fucking life and its daily routine. Arguing with Geza and Gitta about the wallpaper in the entrance hall, menus, electricity bills, what will the boys study after leaving school? Anxiety and insomnia: what are the Israelis up to? Wiesenthal? He broadcasts that his quarry is hiding in Paraguay, according to press reports. Could it be a diversionary tactic to make him lower his guard? The media had claimed that Eichmann was in Kuwait while Mossad was planning his kidnapping in Argentina. Who were those two beefy fellows he met in the forest the other day? And what about Rudel and Barbie, will they betray him? Mengele's missives to Günzburg are more and more distraught: Alois must send more money to the Stammers, as he has done the figures. The bounty on his head of 50,000 marks exceeds the value of his share in the new house. If Geza grasses on him, he'll do well out of it! Mengele complains to Gitta about his family's lack of generosity. Firefighter Sedlmeier intervenes in 1969. He visits Caieiras to give the Stammers a sweetener and pacifies Mengele.

62.

Gerhard visits more frequently now that he has moved closer to São Paulo. One afternoon he is accompanied by a slim middle-aged man with a strong Austrian accent. Wolfram Bossert has short hair and shaved sideburns and is wearing a dark tie with a pristine shirt, and black shoes. He offers pastries to the Stammers, and a hand and an engaging smile to the man introduced as Hochbichler. He is delighted to meet the Swiss farmer whose merits have been so highly praised by his compatriot.

The two Austrians met at the German club in São Paulo a few years previously. A former Wehrmacht corporal, Bossert is another who came to Brazil, to El Dorado, following the defeat of the Reich. As maintenance manager at a paper works, he may not be a spectacular success, but he has done better than his compatriot. A great lover of classical music, he is nicknamed 'Musikus', Bossert has intellectual and artistic pretensions that he loves to share with others. He could be a distraction for Mengele in his moribund existence.

Gerhard was so insistent that the war criminal meet Bossert, he finally agreed, with the provision his own true identity is not revealed. As they enjoy tea, Mengele stares at and tests the stranger. His origins and record are unimpressive, but this is offset by his being cultured and having seemingly faultless beliefs: racist, anti-Semitic and reactionary, Bossert recites his breviary of hate without hitting any false notes. He is a Nazi fanatic, another lost soldier of Hitler, 'the greatest German of all times', he announces enthusiastically. 'Germany at its peak . . .' He returns with Gerhard several times to Caieiras over the following weeks, and is intrigued by the taciturn Swiss in the bush hat. Hearing the way Hochbichler speaks, with an ill-concealed Bavarian accent, and his accurate reflections on history and biology, Bossert assumes that he is not just anyone. Mengele remains on guard even though the company of Musikus is pleasant: he could be an Israeli sleeper agent, a brilliant actor, a crooked informer. Gerhard does not agree. He knows the man's 'charming' wife Liselotte, who 'between you and me, doctor, has a great arse', and his two young children, Sabine and Andreas. Mengele has nothing to fear and should even come clean about his true identity. Gerhard has already discussed it with Sedlmeier, who gave his assent after meeting the technician briefly during his last visit to Brazil. Mengele unmasks reluctantly; Bossert must swear in front of Gerhard, upon the heads of his children, that he will not reveal the secret to anyone.

63.

For the first time since his arrival in Brazil, Mengele has begun to venture outside. Every Wednesday evening, jittery with excitement, he smooths back his hair, dresses in his best clothes and conceals a revolver in his raincoat pocket before going to the Bosserts' house for dinner. The first few times, Gerhard went with him, since Mengele feared an ambush. Now, Musikus comes to pick him up at 7 p.m. sharp. If there's not too much traffic, they can reach the bland bungalow in the suburbs of São Paulo in twenty minutes. Inside, it is a Germanic domain of severe family portraits, Alpine trinkets and Gmunden earthenware pottery, where Bossert's wife and well-trained children warmly welcome their Uncle Peter. Mengele is the centre of attention. For him, this place is an oasis where, for a few hours, he can forget the Stammers, his miserable life and his fear. He teaches Sabine and Andreas how to play Monopoly, then shamelessly asks for several helpings of liver dumpling soup before Musikus nervously carves the pork roast. It is a great honour for him and his wife to entertain the man who collected blue eyes, the most famous living Nazi on the planet. As soon as the meal is over, Liselotte goes to the kitchen to wash dishes, while the two men adjourn to the living room and listen to classical music.

They have an intense discussion. Or rather Bossert sips a schnapps and pulls on his porcelain pipe while his guest moans about his fate and pours out bile: Aryans, Jewish reptiles, biological superiority, the proud and heroic German people . . . Mengele rolls out his usual litany of old ideas and obsessions and airs his predatory, fretful concerns about the world faced with a degenerating Germany and an Austria led respectively by 'the deserter Brandt and the Jew Kreisky'. 'Forced sterilization and the elimination of unproductive elements are essential in order to reduce the demographics of the most primitive and to preserve and refine the purity and innocence of natural selection after millennia of Judaeo-Christian alienation.' The Austrian corporal approves, and hesitates before making a note of the words of the genetic engineer, whom he flatters slavishly. To spend time with a scholar of such calibre is a great opportunity to learn. Mengele has found the disciple he's been looking for since Haase died in Buenos Aires ten years ago – Krug, and now Gerhard, are but contemptible aides de camp. Mörike, Novalis, Spengler . . . Musikus follows his reading recommendations to the letter. The same goes for records. He begins a study of Hellenism and botany. He even develops a fascination for cockroaches. Musikus fervently admires the old Nazi, and Mengele enjoys the influence he exerts on this docile and punctual man, so very different from the Stammers, who mock his whims while robbing him of his fortune. Barbarians: he spits on the Hungarian family every Wednesday evening. Best not to interrupt or contradict him. Bossert had the misfortune of doing so once, suggesting it was in his own best interest to take into account the Stammers' good qualities. Mengele cut short their conversation with a crazed look in his eyes.

Musikus escorts him back to Caieiras shortly before midnight. He is struck by the sudden change in him as they prepare to leave. The arrogant, talkative guest sinks into silence, firmly settles his wide-brimmed hat on his head, and pulls up the collar of his coat, trembling; his features tense. He breaks into a sweat at the sight of a policeman, and in the car he hides his face in his hands, diving headfirst to tie his shoelaces when a vehicle stops level with theirs at a red light. As soon as he leaves Bossert's home, Mengele reverts to a hunted creature.

Yet he agrees to go with his friends for a weekend in the jungle, and allows Musikus to photograph him, the first time he's let anyone do so since the late 1950s. Bossert tries to convince him that he is unrecognisable, and encourages him to leave his self-imposed solitary confinement – otherwise he will come to a bad end. 'He might as well commit suicide', he said to his wife after taking Mengele back to Caieiras one night. What about his prominent forehead? The space between his two upper front teeth? Bossert insists he will not be at risk if he avoids attention. A slow rehabilitation begins. Protected by Gerhard and Musikus, Mengele allows himself to go on brief excursions away from the Stammers, even forgoing his hat and raincoat when the weather warms up. The fugitive slips incognito into the city, the Bossert children going with him on the bus to the supermarket and the cinema. He sweats and shakes for fear of being recognised by a survivor of Auschwitz, or by an irritating physiognomist. He grits his teeth, is a little more self-assured, and sometimes dreams of leading a less shackled life in his old age. His family gives in to another whim and helps him to buy a studio in São Paulo, from which he will receive rental income. But business is business: the property title deed is in the name of Miklos Stammer.

64.

The day after his sixtieth birthday, he has a stomach ache. The severe cramps might have been caused by Liselotte's cheese tart, which had spoiled in the heat, or else by stress: at the party, Gerhard told him in a quavering voice he would be leaving Brazil soon, forever. He is struggling financially, and his wife and son might be seriously ill. They must undergo a series of examinations, blood tests, X-rays, bone-marrow biopsies, and they would prefer to do this in Austria, where the health system is better. 'But what about me?' Mengele asks. Bossert will be his new babysitter; he will forward Mengele's mail, do his shopping, and act as an intermediary between Günzburg and the Stammers. Gerhard offers Mengele his ID card as a farewell gift. All he has to do is replace the photograph with his own – easily done – and Musikus can help him laminate the document. It will be useful for dealing with bureaucratic formalities. The one he has in Hochbichler's name is a badly made fake that could eventually cause him problems.

The stomach ache returns a few months later; the pain is piercing and excruciating. Mengele is suffering from colic. He places a bag of ice on his abdomen, then a green clay pack made with warm water, and fasts for a whole day, but nothing doing; not even the hawthorn herbal tea or the drugs and antibiotics that Bossert buys for him are a help. It gets worse: diarrhoea gives way to bloating, vomiting, severe constipation; his gut is blocked, and his body weakens; swellings appear on his neck, he gets a fever. On waking one morning, Mengele presses his belly and discovers a lump. He immediately thinks it is a tumour, or else the Stammers have poisoned him to get their hands on the house, the studio, and his notebooks, which they will sell for a fortune to a publisher. He writhes in pain but rejects the suggestion of a doctor's visit. 'It's too dangerous,' he whispers to Bossert, who is by his bedside. Geza is against it too, as he fears the likely complications that a visit could cause, and, besides, he does not believe in the complaint. Their guest is a foxy old hypochondriac who will recover as he always does. But this time it is serious. Mengele can no longer eat, he drinks with difficulty and the atrocious taste of shit befouls his mouth. Still lucid, he realises that the vomiting and smell of shit in his nose are signs of peritonitis, and the abscess could burst. It is an emergency and he must consult a specialist. Bossert drives him to the hospital in São Paulo.

The doctor palpates the belly of the seemingly moribund man, who moans. He looks at the marble face, the snowy moustache and the lined forehead, and checks his record based on the papers provided by Bossert on arrival in the admissions department. The X-rays will give a diagnosis. The doctor is puzzled. In all his twenty years as a medic, he says, he has never seen a white patient whose body is in such a bad state at the age of just forty-six or forty-seven. Mr Gerhard has not had an easy life. Musikus suddenly remembers that the date of birth inscribed on Mengele's real-fake ID card is 1925, not 1911. He claims it is a mistake made by the hospital administration, which he will correct; hats off to you, doctor, the patient is in fact ten years older. Opportunely a nurse arrives, images in hand. 'All will be well, Wolfgang, it'll be fine', Bossert says to his furious guru.

A dark, round object the size of a billiard ball is blocking his gut. Cancer? No, an intestinal obstruction. Has he swallowed a foreign object? No, he has not eaten for days, and the pain first began a year ago. So what . . . ? It is a mystery, but he needs an operation, immediately.

The doctor removes an impressive hairball from Mengele's belly. After nervously chewing his moustache for years and years, he has ingested enough hair to form an enmeshed mass that has clogged his intestines. A close shave, in every sense. 'Wolfgang Gerhard' pays his hospital bill in cash and vanishes into thin air.

65.

Mengele is shaken. His surgical wound heals but his strength continues to wane. His worn body gives worrying signs. He winds up with impacted vertebrae after routinely lifting a log, and the migraines that assail him are so intense that he sometimes has to take to his bed for several days and lie in the dark. His prostate swells, his sight fails, and he is tortured by toothache. At the end of 1972, using a piece of string and a knife, he pulls out a molar with its filling that threatens to infect his lower gum. The pain is unbearable, pounding at the pulp and enamel like a hammer and tongs; his nerves scream. Mengele avoids seeing a dentist, as he is still traumatised by the hospital doctor's remark about his date of birth. Gerhard's ID card was a poisoned chalice. He knows full well that he is paying for the stress, the loneliness and the sleepless nights of the past ten years; for the arduous manual labour done in direct sunlight; for the humiliations and arguments, separations, heat, melancholy and damp; and for his shrivelled heart. His morbid ideas and existential angst return, along with the shadow of death. He is in despair about the Stammers' indifference to his distress.

He relies solely on Musikus, his last ally. But Bossert is not Gerhard. He does not leap into his Volkswagen at the slightest wail. He is not as dedicated or as fanatical as his compatriot.

Although he admires the fugitive's pig-headedness, he keeps him at a distance, and will not sacrifice either his career or his family. Mengele is a narcissistic manipulator. Bossert is struck by his callous attitude towards Gerhard, who has endured a series of calamities: the medical examinations in Austria revealed that his wife was suffering from stomach cancer and his son Adolf from bone cancer. Treatments would cost a fortune. Gerhard turned to his former protégé, from whom he had never claimed a centavo for his loyal decade of service. But Mengele snorted, convinced that Gerhard was racketeering by inflating the medical costs: it would be better to accept the inevitable in the short term, namely the death of his wife, rather than squander other people's money! If Bossert hadn't insisted, Mengele would not have asked his brother to help Gerhard. Even so, Bossert thinks to himself, he would not have done it had he not feared that his former retainer would in desperation sell his secrets to a reporter or to the police. True to himself, Mengele then wrote to Gerhard that he was shocked by the miserliness of his family.

The old Nazi pushes against the limits of his entourage. In the early 1970s, he irritates his last loyal supporters by lamenting his fate and interfering in the private lives of his relatives, giving unwanted advice, constantly clamouring for their attention (and money and letters), like a child. Martha rarely writes to him. Alois finds the way he criticises his management of the family business intolerable and resents his advice on the education of his son, Dieter, whom Josef does not even know. The fugitive asks to see the list of blacklisted families in Günzburg, should Dieter ever want to get married. Alois also asks him to stop sending their nephew Karl-Heinz long missives in which he pours out all his frustrations, praising the Führer and eugenics and vilifying the German Federal Republic, which has been so tolerant of the family. The world order has changed. After his father's death, in 1974, Dieter refuses to answer the solicitations of his uncle in South America. Even loyal Sedlmeier is getting sick of commuting back and forth to Brazil, weary of the endless grievances and Mengele's obdurate mindset, his constant quarrels with the Stammers, and his lack of gratitude. No other Nazi on the run has benefited from so much support!

Mengele has become a burden, but the Günzburg family cannot abandon him, for if he were arrested, public knowledge of such a firm family bond with the Angel of Death would be the undoing of their business, which is now a multinational, with a turnover of millions of marks and more than two thousand employees. In 1971, Sedlmeier lies to an investigating judge while testifying under oath: Mengele has no relationship with his family; he has never worked for the company; he very likely lives in Paraguay: Sedlmeier reads the newspapers like everyone else. He last bumped into him at Buenos Aires airport over ten years ago.

66.

Rolf Mengele is a tormented young man. Whenever he introduces himself, he is greeted by an embarrassed silence and
furtive looks. Mengele, like . . . ? Yes, Mengele. The son of
Satan. Damned patronymic: his cross and his banner. He will
never forget his consternation and his sorrow the day when,
while reading the newspapers shortly after the kidnapping of
Eichmann, he discovered that the uncle who amused him
with stories about gauchos and Indians at Hotel Engel was in
fact his father, the Auschwitz torturer. A deadly family. Raised
by his mother, Rolf became a lawyer in Freiburg and fled from
the Günzburg clan. He despises the Mengeles' clannish
silence over his father's crimes and their disdain for his
victims. Their insular solidarity, their greed and their coward-
ice are odious. Rolf positions himself to the Left in the fight
against capitalism and fascism, and the hypocritical attempts
of Mercedes-Benz and other companies that had benefitted
from the Nazi regime to appease the conscience of good West
German society. Rolf takes part in the protest movement of
the post-war period; his cousins Dieter and Karl-Heinz nickname him 'the Communist'. He is a rebel but a fragile one:
snared in contradictions; tortured by the heavy burden of his
toxic father.

At the Pinakothek in Munich, standing in front of the jumble of naked bodies portrayed in Rubens's *The Fall of the Damned*, he cannot help but think about his father standing on the selection ramp, the great orchestrator of the macabre ballet, a demon in immaculate uniform who hurried men into the darkness. If only he had died in Russia, as the family legend had claimed . . . If only he, Rolf, had the courage to send him packing, to announce his marriage to a Polish Jewess or a Zairian rather than a German from a good family, and his plan to settle in a kibbutz as one of her good friends; if only he could find the strength to deliver him to the courts. But Rolf cannot. It would be parricide, creating more torment and additional drama. His father is Josef Mengele. He is the son of Josef Mengele. Rolf has to know: Why? How? The selections? The experiments? Auschwitz? Does the old man feel no regret at all, no remorse? Is he the cruel beast described in the newspapers? Is he so very malign and degenerate? Can Rolf help him save his soul? And he, Rolf, is he made bad by the sins of his father?

In the early 1970s, father and son intensify their correspondence. Mengele neglected Rolf for a long time because the boy hid beneath Irene's petticoats. He prefers Karl-Heinz, the spiritual son he remembers as a model teenager while living by his side in Argentina. But since his brush with death, Mengele has got it into his head that he has to reconnect with the biological son he spent ten days with in Switzerland, fifteen years ago. He expects to receive from him the compassion that the others refuse to give. He spares him none of his daily worries nor his health troubles – sinusitis; damaged discs, 'the beginning of osteoarthritis of the spine' – hoping that Rolf will feel sorry for him, knowing how much more fragile and sensitive his son is compared with all the other Mengeles. Emotional blackmail, massaging his pride, scheming. The father purposely extols to his son the qualities of his cousin Karl-Heinz, 'a remarkable German', 'hard-working, modest and affectionate, he regularly sends me money behind Alois's back, and Dieter's too', and Rolf would 'do well to follow suit'. He wants to train the greenhorn, his lost son, led astray by 'the Jewish media which has sold out to money and power' thanks to his lax education at the hands of Irene and the shoe merchant from Freiburg. 'Without author-ity, the world is discordant and existence is incomprehensible', he writes. Mengele criticises Rolf's way of life, disparages his wife's looks, and does not bother to respond to his emotional setbacks – Rolf divorced only a year after getting married. When the young man gives up on finishing his thesis, Mengele is contemptuous of his son's lack of ambition: 'Everybody was a lawyer in our day. If you want me to be proud of you, get your law degree.' Mengele then softens and pleads for a sign of affec-tion – photos, postcards of the Black Forest and Munich. He is so unhappy and lonely 'in the jungle, banished to the other side of the world'.

Rolf struggles, gives in, challenges, questions: but what about Auschwitz, *Dad*? Mengele pronounces himself innocent of the crimes of which he is accused. He fought to defend 'incontro-vertible traditional values' and never killed anyone. Quite the contrary, by deciding who was fit to work, he saved lives. He feels no guilt. Rolf has been misinformed, he has to draw a line

under certain painful events: going endlessly over the past is
unhealthy. Germany was in danger of being destroyed. After
all, a father and son must love each other, whatever the circumstances. He asks him to visit him in Brazil. 'Keep an open mind,
without preconceptions.'

Rolf ponders. Deep down, he knows he will only get peace
of mind by facing his parent, the doctor smiling and whistling
opera arias on the selection ramp at Auschwitz. Face to face,
man to man, Mengele vs. Mengele. They are beginning to plan
the trip when a new drama erupts with the Stammers.

67.

Mengele hits Gitta. A silly argument that escalated, over the last
square of chocolate, a broken jar of jam, his hand on the
buttocks of the former dancer. The cause is unclear, but Gitta
screams and Mengele slaps her. Geza grabs hold of the decrepit
Nazi and immediately telephones Bossert. Mengele has to go.
He must stay with his friends for the time it takes Sedlmeier to
cross the Atlantic. For once, the Stammers are inflexible: even
the $5,000 which is waved under their noses leaves them cold.
After thirteen years of cohabiting, it's time to get a divorce.
Goodbye, Peter; goodbye, Hochbichler, and good riddance.
What do we do with Mengele? Musikus does not have
Gerhard's connections. Rudel has flown the coop. Alternatives

176

are running out. The close friend who agreed to take him ducks out. He has not been able to sleep at night, convinced he is being followed by an anonymous unknown person ever since Musikus entrusted him with the plan. Bossert's wife, Liselotte, does not like the way Mengele scrutinises her legs and bottom as soon as her back is turned. He swears that he cannot allow Mengele to come and sow discord in his home.

Time is running out; the Stammers have already sold Caieiras and moved into a sumptuous 1,000-square-metre villa in São Paulo. Mengele and Cigano have two months to vacate the premises, otherwise they will be out on the street by the end of January 1975. Without a means of escape, the sexagenarian contemplates the unthinkable: he will live alone for the first time since leaving Buenos Aires. Geza decides to make him pay a hefty price for his affair with Gitta and inflicts a final humiliation on him. The old man has bought a bungalow with his share of the sale of Caieiras: now he must pay Geza rent to live there. It is a stucco hovel in Eldorado, an impoverished suburb of São Paulo. Mengele has no legal recourse.

The Fall. He has vertigo when Bossert deposits him at his new home like a bottle being dropped off at the dump and vanishes without a word, an embarrassed smile on his lips. The door closes. Cigano barks. Mengele staggers; despairing, he imagines the trapdoor to the damp cellar below as leading to the abyss. He tells himself the next stop will be the cemetery or prison. So much for El Dorado! The bungalow in Alvarenga Street is gloomy, the walls are covered with mould, the bathroom is shabby and tiny, the cooker is a portable butane-gas stove, the roof leaks. So much for El Dorado! Is this where the eugenicist from a good family ends up? His last base is in a chaotic enclave of mulattoes. Brazil's underbelly is about to swallow him up.

For the first few months, he plans to brighten up the hovel and make it more secure. But his solitude saps his energy. He starts tiling the bathroom and tinkering in the kitchen without finishing anything. Lying naked on the concrete floor, his revolver within reach, he fixates on the revolving fan blades for hours, forgetting about the bars at the windows which he has started to install. Ever since his childhood he has been an early riser – now he gets up late. Sometimes he goes back to bed, his throat tight. What's the point, he mutters to Cigano, how many more hard knocks do I have to take? Everything he does fails as though he were cursed. The water which filters through the device he has fixed on the roof still tastes of iron; however much he airs his room it has a musty smell; and the cockroaches that proliferate there no longer excite him. When the sun goes down, he is overcome with sadness . . . Irene . . . Martha . . . He longs for a gesture of comfort; sometimes he even misses the Stammers. He only ever sees them to settle their accounts: Hello, the rent of the bungalow minus the rent of the studio that is his, Goodbye and thank you. Gitta waits in the car while Geza fetches the money. Only Bossert brings him relief. He comes to dinner every Wednesday, listens to Bach and Mengele's lamentations, his perpetual grievances, Germany, Hitler, family, health. His blood pressure is too high. He suffers from rheumatism and insomnia; he is fearful of needing an operation for his prostate; he is appalled by the state of his back – his vertebrae are so damaged that he walks with difficulty. 'Rolf is weak, Sedlmeier is selfish, Rudel is a turncoat materialist and Dieter a son of a bitch like his father, that dog Alois.' And Alois does not send enough money; luckily, Karl-Heinz supplements his meagre pension, though the end of the month is still difficult; he was hesitant about buying a tape recorder. And Mengele talks about his new obsession, the disreputable *barrio* into which Providence has thrown him – 'a den of blacks and mulattoes, thieves and junkies' – where 'garbage piles up and rats proliferate'. 'The other night, some riffraff rang the bell in the middle of the night and I couldn't get back to sleep. It's a nightmare,' moans the boy from Günzburg to Musikus: insane traffic, electricity cuts, motorcycles backfiring, filth, shacks built from odds and ends, insecurity, a muddle. Weekend binges and collective ecstasy on match or *macumba* nights . . . Such decay . . . 'I cannot believe I have fallen so low.'

In the eyes of the neighbourhood, Mengele is Pedro, an eccentric and deranged old man. He has not left the area since a couple eyeballed him in the subway – or rather he thought that a man whispering in the ear of a woman stared at him. Mengele is mired in paranoia, he is obsessed with his prominent forehead, the space between his two upper front teeth; every time he ventures head down to the grocery store, the stray Cigano at his heels, he quakes at the idea of being unmasked, sworn at, captured, beaten up. The newspapers he buys every day endlessly write about him; they are obsessive, and he is

179

stunned, he cannot get over it, the mythical tales describing him as being all-powerful in the Paraguayan jungle in Pedro Juan Caballero, or wealthy in Peru; that damned Wiesenthal claims to have missed him by a hair's breadth in Spain; a bounty of tens of thousands of dollars is on offer for his capture; and a Hollywood movie is being filmed, he reads. *Marathon Man*, in which Laurence Olivier plays the White Angel, a Nazi dentist 'loosely based on the dreaded Dr Mengele, the Angel of Death at Auschwitz, who is still on the run'. But in reality he is a wreck, unable to remember what the women who loved him look like, reduced to moping about at home and jumping out of his skin when a cat mews. He who is invisible and in agony and would yell to the world if he could that he is sick and all alone like a dog, will die alone in the rubble of the *favela*. Everyone runs away from him. Everyone avoids him – even little Luis, the local sixteen-year-old gardener. For a while they liked to tend to their flowers together, talk about botany while eating ice cream under the cannonball trees in the municipal square behind the bungalow. Pedro thought that Luis liked him: he opened the front door to his lair, offered him sweets and chocolate, and taught him about classical music. He bought a television to please him.

But the youngster got scared when the old moustachioed man waltzed alone before him, and suggested he stay the night: they could watch soap operas together and build a hut in the garden the next day. Luis never came back.

68.

Bossert alerts Sedlmeier in the autumn of 1975 that Brazil is about to change the format of its ID cards. Gerhard has to return to São Paulo, since only he can apply for a replacement card in accordance with the new legislation. Mengele cannot turn up at the administrative offices. Sedlmeier has to convince the Austrian to do this last service for his old friend. It is a sensitive mission; Gerhard is overwrought and dead set against Mengele, who was reluctant to pay for his wife's treatment and that of his son. The fugitive also refused to finance the photographic-equipment shop that he was planning to open in Austria. He asked for 30,000 marks but got only 1,000, and only after some bitter negotiations. In the meantime, his wife has died and young Adolf has not been given the all-clear. Gerhard needs money, but also respect. Sedlmeier realises that to grease his palm will not be sufficient. So he'll pick him up in the Mercedes and take him to Braunau am Inn to enjoy luncheon in the best restaurant in town, where it all began. Hitler was born in a house in Salzburger Vorstadt, which they visit after a lavish lunch and some big cigars. The fanatic is moved to tears, and Sedlmeier takes the opportunity to unveil his plan: in memory of the Führer, he will return in Brazil, renew his identity card and save SS Capt. Mengele.

Gerhard arrives in São Paulo early in 1976.

There is nothing difficult about switching or faking the cards, but Mengele's looks less genuine than it did before, since he is now so wrinkled. It pains Gerhard to see him like this: a haggard, unshaven old man. The Austrian helps him redecorate his living room and hangs a stuffed boar's head in his bedroom, but now he must return to Europe to look after his sick son. Gerhard asks Bossert to devote more time to their friend, or to introduce him to a family who can come and entertain him from time to time. Musikus thinks of Ernesto Glawe, an Argentine textile engineer of German origin. 'A decent man,' Gerhard agrees. 'He'll do.' Before Gerhard leaves, he introduces Glawe to the old man. It would be madness to reveal Pedro Gerhard's true identity, however, so Glawe is informed that he is a former military doctor who served on the Russian front, a distant relative of Wolfgang Gerhard's.

Gerhard has calmly completed the last mission entrusted to him by Sedlmeier about which Bossert is kept informed: he has booked a resting place for a sick uncle next to his mother's grave in the cemetery in Embu das Artes. Gerhard never sees Mengele again. He collapses in front of his car in 1978, at age fifty-three.

69.

Mengele spends Sunday, 16 May 1976, in the company of Glawe. For the first time ever, he joins in the ritual gathering of the *asado*, which is so much more than just a barbecue. Usually Ernesto and his son Norberto visit the old man with packets of cookies and prepared dishes in a covered basket – Bossert having warned them that Uncle Pedro lacks an appetite and does not know how to cook. Despite the arbour in the garden, Mengele is suffocating on this flaming-hot Sunday, and he asks Norberto to accompany him home before the coffee is served. He is apologetic, saying he is on the verge of getting one of his appalling migraines, and no, he does not want to lie down, he wants to get home as soon as possible. 'Thank you, little one.' Back at his front door, he cannot open it; how odd, he does not have the strength to turn the key in the lock. His right arm is numb and will not respond to the orders sent by his brain, which suddenly hurts atrociously; it is as though a valve has opened and his mind is flooded. There are internal explosions, and he is unable to call for help, to articulate his words or to see clearly. He limps back to Norberto's car panic-stricken and vomits; his lower lip hangs lopsidedly to the right. He is hospitalised for fifteen days. Mengele recovers slowly from his stroke. Bossert and Glawe take turns at his bedside.

When he returns home from the clinic, Norberto moves in, since Uncle Pedro is not fit to live alone. According to the doctors he is very lucky: the stroke has caused little permanent damage.

The cohabitation of the young South American and the exhausted Nazi sours fast. Norberto has neither the patience nor the nursing skills to cope with Pedro's devouring anxiety or his mad rage when his memory plays tricks on him. He hurls aside the screwdriver or the book that his floppy right hand can no longer hold, and complains about how the spaghetti has been cooked. After a sleepless night when the old man dreams and yells in German, Norberto decides to clear off. The Glawe family never wants to see him again.

'*Housekeeper required, good cook, patient and dedicated care-taker for an elderly gentleman. References required. Only serious applicants . . .*' An angular woman of about thirty years of age answers Bossert's classified ad. Elsa Gulpian de Oliveira enters into service with Don Pedro in late 1976.

70.

Punctual and smiling, Elsa airs, scours and dusts Mengele's hovel from top to bottom. She feels sorry for the old man, always alone, grumbling, nervously biting his nails, reciting German poems to exercise his memory. 'Don Pedro, you shouldn't let yourself go like this.' She encourages him to accompany her when she does the shopping, and Mengele submits, taking the little maid's arm as they go for walks together. Elsa is full of energy and a pretty good cook, too. He takes her out to dinner, invites her to the cinema. Other than Bossert, she is all he has in his life. The day Cigano died she embraced him, sweetly, instinctively; nobody had hugged him like that since Martha. Comforted by Elsa's presence, he starts to feel a little more lively and hopes to keep the promise that he made to himself several years before: to bring his son to Brazil.

In the face of Rolf's procrastination, Mengele sends him pathetic letters with muddled threats and lamentations. He is so lonely and unloved that he will commit suicide if Rolf does not come. He is in a state of collapse, he has nearly died twice; the Israelis are going to murder him. 'Rolf, I need you. We must see each other as soon as possible.'

The tortured young lawyer finally agrees. His father plans his journey as a general would a key battle. Nothing will be left to chance, Rolf must respect all his instructions to get to him, follow multiple false trails, book several hotel rooms, learn to disappear in the crowd and camouflage himself – 'sunglasses and a hat are essential', he says – and to identify a tail and lose his pursuers. 'Rolf, I hope you're in good shape; if not, do some training to prepare for the expedition.' Bossert can give him a weapon when he arrives in São Paulo if he likes. Most importantly, he needs a fake passport. Mengele junior cannot travel under his real name in South America. All are unnecessary precautions: no one is seriously looking for Mengele in the mid-1970s. The West Germans think he is still in Paraguay.

The Israelis do not have up-to-date information and no longer plan to kidnap him. Since the Six Day War, every vote counts in the UN Security Council, including those of Latin American countries, so they avoid harassing them about an old Nazi who may already be dead, and are wary of violating their sovereignty.

Sedlmeier has to oversee the preparations. Woe betide Rolf if he objects in any way! Mengele fulminates, showers him with missives. Rolf wants to travel with a friend whom he trusts, but as Mengele does not know this friend, Rolf must come alone. 'You don't know any of my friends, Daddy,' etc. Dozens of letters cross the Atlantic; time flies. Rolf falls in love in Germany and delays his departure. Mengele is anxious and blames Sedlmeier, who is tearing his hair out. At last, the plane ticket is booked: Rolf will fly on 10 October 1977. Mengele insists that he bring 'nice gifts' for Bossert, convinced that the greed of his family is the reason for his divorce from the Stammers. He wants spare parts for his electric razor, gherkins from Spreewald, and lace doilies for Elsa, to whom he announces the imminent arrival of his nephew. Before his departure, Karl-Heinz and Rolf meet in the Sedlmeiers' garden and Karl-Heinz hands over to his cousin several thousand dollars for him to give to Mengele, the husband of his mother, their dear 'Uncle Fritz'.

Rolf and his friend land safely in Rio de Janeiro. Rolf presents the passport he has pinched from a friend to the border officer. His friend has his valid passport on him, just in case, but the official smiles at him: Welcome to Brazil! After a night in Rio, Rolf takes off alone for São Paulo. As agreed, a taxi drops him off at point A, then a second taxi at point B, and a third at

Bossert's place. The two men head wordlessly for Eldorado and Alvarenga Street. The *favela* stinks of burning meat, wires dangle from the electricity pylons, dogs scavenge in garbage cans. Rolf looks at the shacks, the scruffy men, the plump black women in tank tops. His heart beats wildly. The car jolts to a stop in front of 5555. An old moustachioed man in a short sleeve shirt stands on the threshold, fists on hips.

His father: Josef Mengele.

71.

Rolf is struck by the stuffy smell of the bungalow, and by his father's quavering voice. Formerly virile and imperious, his father had impressed him during their mountain holiday when he was a child. But the young man will not let himself be moved, neither by the old man's tears of welcome, nor by his deformed right hand and his furtive look of a hunted animal. Sedlmeier had warned him, 'Josef is a formidable actor.' Rolf makes him sit down and goes straight to the heart of the matter. After so many years, vague letters and sleepless nights, his father owes him the truth. Why did he go to Auschwitz? What did he actually do there? Is he guilty of the crimes of which he is accused?

For the first time, Mengele is confronted about his monstrous crimes. He coughs as he stares at his son, the spitting image of his mother. The boy is more handsome than in the photos, but

Mengele wishes he did not wear those vile bell-bottomed trousers or have long hair like an American actor – it must be cut while he is in Brazil. He just wants water? But Mengele bought beer and wine in his honour. What about eating something? 'Speak to me, dad, we'll see about the rest later.' Not those old myths? sighs Mengele.

Yes, those old myths

Humanity is a morphology that has no more of a goal or a plan than the orchid or the butterfly. Peoples and languages grow and age just as oaks, pines and flowers do, but humanity itself does not age. All cultures know that new possibilities of expression constantly appear, ripen, fade and never return, says the father, who has prepared for his son's inquisition. After the First World War, the West reached a critical point and Germany, at an inexorable stage of its civilisation, was corrupted by modern technology and capitalism, the masses, individualism and cosmopolitanism. Two options presented themselves: to die or to act. 'We Germans are a superior race, the master race: we had to act. We had to inoculate a new vitality into the natural community to protect it and secure the permanence of the Nordic race for eternity', says Mengele. Hitler envisioned a base of 100 million Germans, 250 million in the medium term and a billion in 2200. 'One billion, Rolf! He was our Caesar, and we, his engineers, were charged with ensuring that he always had a growing number of families which were healthy and racially pure . . .'

Rolf drums his fingers on the table top. He knows Spengler's theories about the decline of the West and did not come all the way to Brazil to hear his father hold forth in the Newspeak of the Nazi catechism. 'Dad, what did you do in Auschwitz?'

Mengele makes a gesture of irritation; he is rarely interrupted. 'My duty,' he says, looking Rolf in the eye. 'My military duty in the name of German science was to protect the organic biological community, purify the blood, eliminate foreign bodies.' He had to sort and eliminate those inferior foreign bodies arriving in their thousands every day at the camp who were unable to work. 'I tried to designate the greatest number able to work, and so I saved the maximum number of lives. The twins, thanks to whom I advanced a scientific cause, owe their lives to me,' he asserts. Rolf looks at him sideways, mystified. Mengele tries to explain the principles of selection: in a military hospital, not all the wounded are operable. Some just die, that's war, that's how the laws of life work: only the strongest survive. When the convoys arrived, they consisted largely of the living dead. What could be done? Auschwitz was not an asylum but a labour camp: better to save them from suffering and annihilate them immediately. 'Believe you me, on some days it was not so easy. Understand?' No, Rolf does not understand, absolutely not, but he does not contradict his father. If he lets him talk, Mengele might make an admission of guilt, express regret. 'I obeyed orders because I loved Germany and respected the policy of its Führer. Of our Führer: legally and morally, I had to fulfil my mission; I had no choice. I did not invent Auschwitz, its gas chambers, its crematoria. I was just one cog among many. *If* certain excesses were committed, I was not responsible. I . . .' Rolf gets up and turns his back on his father. He stops listening, and massages his skull as he looks through the window at some kids playing with a ball.

72.

'The Jews, what did they do to you? The Jews . . . ?' he asks, sitting down again, right in front of his father. Mengele is going on about biology, bacilli, germs and the eradication of larvae. He points to a big mosquito gliding up the wall: 'We would crush him because he is an environmental hazard and a bite could transmit an infection to us. The Jews are the same.' Rolf closes his eyes. He wants to run away but orders his father not to move, they are not done yet; the insect can wait. 'Have you never felt compassion for the children, the women, the old men you sent to the gas chamber? Do you have no remorse?' Mengele gives his son a filthy look. The boy understands nothing, really. 'Mercy is not a valid concept, since the Jews do not belong to the human race,' he says. 'They declared war on us millennia ago; they want to destroy Nordic humanity. We had to eliminate them all. Later, boys would have become men, and girls, mothers, eager for revenge. Today, the survivors poison Germany once again and Israel threatens world peace. Know, Rolf, that conscience is a sickness, invented by morbid humans to inhibit action and paralyse the actors,' says Mengele.

He did not go to court because the judges are only vigilantes and seekers of revenge.

Night falls on Eldorado. Father and son dine in silence. The young man observes the old: a stranger, bursting the yellow yolk of his egg and greedily dipping his bread into it. His moustache is sprinkled with bits of chopped spinach. 'Did you kill, dad? Did you torture and throw newborns into the flames?' Rolf suddenly asks. Mengele sits up straight, looks at him thunderously. He swears he never did harm to anyone, he was just doing his duty as a soldier and a scientist. When a pilot bombs a city in enemy territory, he is not vilified as a criminal by his people. Quite the contrary: he is a treated like a hero. So why is he persecuted by everyone? Anyhow, the Germans never protested, and neither did the Pope. 'It's an unfair calumny,' says Mengele. 'As a surgeon of the people, I worked to secure the future of the Aryan race for eternity and for the happiness of the community. The individual did not count.'

The old man suddenly stands up and yells, his face red, 'You, my only son, you believe in all the lies that are written about me! You petit bourgeois! Influenced by your stupid stepfather, your legal studies and the media, like all your shitty generation. All of this is beyond your understanding, so give me a break. Leave your seniors in peace. Show some respect. I did nothing wrong, Rolf, you hear me?'

It's over. After two days and two nights of relentless discussions, Rolf gives up. His father is stubborn, incurable and evil, a war criminal, a criminal against humanity, unrepentant. It's over, says Rolf. The rest of his visit does not matter: the walks and the photos with Bossert and the picnic on Bertioga Beach are all a sham. He leaves earlier than intended. At the airport, his father mutters that he hopes to see him again.

Rolf walks away towards the boarding area.

73.

Mengele considers his son's visit a triumph. His calmness at the end of his stay was an acquittal of sorts, after such a stormy beginning. Rolf has put a little vitality into him, but four, five, six days after the boy's departure, there is no news of his safe return home. Was he arrested in Rio, or when he landed in Germany? Mengele tried to dissuade him from presenting his real passport on his return to Europe. He writes panicky letters, devours newspapers, watches the news anxiously; perhaps the son of the Angel of Death has been caught returning from Brazil? Mengele bites his nails to the quick until Sedlmeier, one month later, assures him of his son's safe passage. So Rolf's visit served no purpose. The little shit. Mengele is gutted; once again he is overwhelmed by feelings of emptiness and melancholy. Bossert suggests that he move to a better neighbourhood, but the old Nazi does not want to leave Eldorado, since no one would ever think of looking for the most dangerous criminal known to mankind in such a place. Moreover, he has neither the strength nor the desire to familiarise himself with a new environment.

And here, in Eldorado, there is Elsa. She pampers and mothers Mengele on a daily basis. He introduces her to classical music, Latin and Greek; gives her shawls, a gold bracelet and other generous gifts, thanks to Karl-Heinz's money and the sale of the studio in São Paulo. It pains him when his housemaid leaves at the end of the day, standing on tiptoe in front of the bathroom mirror to put on lipstick and go out with other men. When Elsa prepares the coffee in the morning, he looks at her back view and sees Irene; the women are alike, with their slim hips and wavy Venetian-blonde hair swept up in a bun. Elsa is fond of Don Pedro, who reminds her of her father, who died when she was fifteen. He treats her well. He is distinguished and so very different from the drunken brutes hovering around her in the neighbourhood.

Don Pedro accompanies her to her sister's wedding. He refuses to pose for family photos but dances willingly with the young woman, pressed right up against her slender body, inhaling her breath tinged with lime and *cachaça*. The old man desires her. Shortly before midnight, Mengele pretends he has a sudden backache and shooting pain down one leg, so she walks him home.

Elsa massages Don Pedro's desiccated body. His right thigh hurts. When the gullible young woman reaches out a hand, Mengele guides it to his penis. Elsa complains. 'For the principle of the thing', he thinks to himself as he squeezes her wrist. Elsa gives in as she always does, anxious to please Don Pedro. She begins to stroke the shaft, to play with it tenderly, then shake it more energetically, but it does not swell and stiffen;

quite the contrary, it curls up like a snail. Mengele is insistent –
'gently', 'faster' – but he does not get an erection. What a
disaster. The housemaid strokes his hair and cradles him like
the son she does not yet have: yes, she will happily sleep in Don
Pedro's bed tonight.

The next morning, he asks Elsa to move in with him. She
refuses. 'It's not done, Don Pedro, what will the neighbours
say . . . My mother? We are a poor but respectable family.' Or, if
she were to do so, it would be on condition that they marry.

74.

'No, it isn't possible. It's impossible,' splutters Mengele, helpless,
bursting into tears. He would like it, he would love it, if this
gentle, caring woman were to become his wife and share his
last years. But he cannot tell her that he is crippled by fear at
the idea of presenting Gerhard's genuine fake papers to the
Municipal Civil Registrar for Eldorado. Elsa, also in tears,
makes the sign of the cross three times, and hides her face in
her hands. If he has nothing to add and cannot even give her an
explanation, she'll leave. She's not a whore. Don Pedro may be
a good man, but he will have to hire a new housemaid.

The old Nazi refuses to let go of his last ally. He visits her
mother. Swears that he will give Elsa a pay rise and the best life
possible. He kneels and clasps his hands before his chest,

crushed by feelings of suffocation. He begs her to persuade her daughter to come back to work for him. 'Then marry her.' Accursed conventions! The vileness of Catholicism! Mengele is desperate. He harasses them, lurks in front of their shack, sends them flowers; he wails, pleads and moans. Don Pedro is a strange old man. The mother tells the girl that he has lost his mind and she would do well to stay away from him. In October 1978, Elsa announces to Mengele that she is going to get married and that he has to leave her alone. He collapses, begs her to renounce such a plan, protests that no man could ever care for her as well as he could. But she will hear none of it. 'I will die soon,' Don Pedro mutters.

Elsa's departure is the final blow. Mengele's precarious health is deteriorating rapidly, despite the arrival of a new maid, Inez, who moves into a shed at the end of the garden. His body is giving out: he has hives, shingles and problems with his liver. He has no appetite and is visibly losing weight; his life is meaningless, and he is tortured by loneliness; he has lost his fighting spirit, he writes to Sedlmeier, and since everyone has abandoned him, he is ready to commit suicide. His nights are atrocious as he is devoured by terrors that crush his ribcage; he has burning pains as if he were going to suffocate. Eyes closed, on his knees, before going to sleep, he says the prayer in Latin that his father recited to him to soothe him: *Procul recedant somnia et noctium phantasmata*. May our sleep be free from nightmares. But nothing can save his soul or appease his troubles. Mengele no longer sleeps. He asks Inez to leave the light on in the living room, as if for a child. He goes to her garden

195

shed to wish her good night; if only she would agree to sleep with him, he could rest for a few hours at long last. Sometimes he hears voices and wanders through the bungalow at night like a sleepwalker, looking for his ghosts. Dementia prowls ever closer. By day, he bumps into furniture and mumbles to himself, Rolf, Irene, *Papa*. He does not even have the strength to celebrate Christmas Eve with the Bossert family. When Musikus drops by on the morning of the twenty-fifth bringing him left-over meat and a piece of cake, the old man has a greyish tinge and is dozing in a pool of urine and excrement. A box of suppositories lies on the bedside table, alongside nail clippings and a greeting card: Sedlmeier wishes him a Happy New Year 1979 and tells him that he has been a grandfather for a few months. Rolf did not send an announcement of the birth of his son.

In January, there is a heat wave across the state of São Paulo. Bossert suggests to Mengele that he leave his oven and come to the Bossert holiday home in Bertioga where he can cool off by the ocean. The children will be happy to see their uncle. On 7 February 1979, Mengele boards a bus at dawn destined for the port of Santos. Musikus picks up the listless old man, who is in a foul mood, at the bus station. Exhausted, Mengele does not eat lunch and locks himself in his room to have a nap. He dreams. For the first time in many moons, Mengele dreams.

75.

A forest wreathed in mist, hazy countryside, crying and sighing in a jumble of languages, uncouth jargon . . . crowds of naked children, women and men, plagued by flies and wasps, are escorted by black devils . . . Eichmann, Rudel, Gitta and Geza Stammer, and von Verschuer, the unscrupulous geneticist, are among the prisoners, along with the whole Günzburg clan: the venerable family is reunited – father, mother, brothers, wives, sons and nephews each push a block of granite as they curse themselves. A huge fire is being prepared. Goats and monkeys pull carts loaded with wood. An orchestra tunes its instruments. A dishevelled witch up on a platform harangues the cortège, her arms raised to the stars and to the threatening slow-laden clouds. It is the eve of Carnival and the goddess Germania is about to be martyred.

'Mengele!' yell two hoarse voices. 'Mengele!' He turns. Two men in rags take aim. He recognises the father and son he had dissected and boiled at Auschwitz, two humble Jews from Łódź, the hunchbacked father and his crippled son. They come forward and point their pistols at the temple of the old doctor in his immaculate lab coat. Mengele shudders, kneels, pleads. The hunchback bursts out laughing, and the cripple whistles an aria from *Tosca*.

76.

He wakes up exhausted and bathed in sweat. His heart is pounding and he is trembling from head to toe. On this seventh day of February 1979 he senses that he is reaching the end of his macabre journey.

Despite his backache, he manages to get up and put on his bathing trunks. Without drinking or eating anything, he goes down to the beach below the holiday home. Bossert waves a hand in greeting. Would he like to lie beneath the parasol? How about a glass of lemonade, a salted cod fritter? Mengele suggests they walk along the shoreline instead. Head and chest bared to the blinding sunlight, he advances in a daze, ignoring Bossert's banal chit-chat. He feels breathless and his head starts to spin; he has to sit down on a rock. Silence. For a moment, everything hangs in suspension: children's voices, a flight of birds, the sound of the surf and the bracing sea wind that whips up the pale sand. Suddenly Mengele begins to speak, babbling on about ruins, his parents, Günzburg, as he stares at the horizon. He dreams of going home to end his days, he says. He is dying of thirst and heat here.

He is just dying. Impelled by some mysterious force, he goes all alone into the turquoise water and floats head down, no longer aware of his aching body or his rotten organs, as he is carried by the current out into the deep blue sea, until suddenly his scraggy neck stiffens, his jaws tighten, his limbs freeze, he groans, and seagulls beat their wings and glide overhead, squawking joyfully as Mengele drowns. He is still breathing when Bossert battles the waves to bring him back to the shore, but it is a corpse that he drags out of the sea.

'Uncle Pedro is dead!' Liselotte and the children exclaim. Uncle Pedro died in the immensity of the ocean, in the Brazilian sun, sneakily, without ever having faced the justice of men or answered to his victims for his unspeakable crimes.

Mengele is interred the following day under his false identity in Embu das Artes. Bossert, who is in hospital, misses the funeral. Only his wife, the funeral director and a crematorium assistant witness the burial of 'Wolfgang Gerhard'.

EPILOGUE

The Ghost

77.

On 27 January 1985, snow falls on Auschwitz. It is the fortieth anniversary of the liberation of the camp. Among the survivors who have come in commemoration of that day there is a group of twins, dwarves and cripples in their fifties and sixties. The survivors of Mengele's human zoo call for justice in front of the cameras. Their appeal is broadcast around the world as they urge governments to capture their torturer at last. 'We know he is alive. He must pay the price.'

Most of them fly from Poland back to Israel. On 4 February, a mock trial for the war criminal is staged at Yad Vashem's Holocaust Memorial in Jerusalem. Sitting at the head of the tribunal are the chief prosecutor from the Jerusalem trial of Eichmann, the Nazi-hunter Simon Wiesenthal, and the chief US military counsel from the Nuremberg war crimes trial. For three consecutive days, Mengele's human guinea pigs testify to their torturing. A former guard from the Gypsy Block recalls the experiments on Gypsy twins. After injecting sperm from a male into a female twin hoping the young woman will give birth to yet more twins, Mengele observes that she is carrying only one child; he promptly snatches the baby from the uterus and throws it into the fire. Benumbed, another woman says that she should have killed her little eight-day-old daughter. She relives her anguish as Mengele gives the order for her chest to be bound up to deprive her child of milk: he wants to know how long a newborn can go without feeding. Another mother hears her baby screaming and screaming, and eventually injects him with morphine provided by a Jewish doctor. Women describe how SS guards shatter the skulls of living newborns with their rifle butts and describe Mengele's office wall as having eyes pinned to it like butterflies. The testimonies are broadcast worldwide, and the repercussions are immense. Even before the end of trial, the US attorney general demands that the complete file be reviewed and calls for the arrest of the war criminal. Pressure is applied by the Simon Wiesenthal Center in Los Angeles, which has just released a declassified counter-intelligence memorandum indicating that the Americans held Mengele in 1947. The information is incorrect, but it provokes an uproar: did the Americans allow the Angel of Death to slip through their fingers? Did they use his services as they did those of so many other Nazis after the war? The Office of Special Investigations created by the Carter administration to track down Nazi criminals in the United States coordinates the investigation. The CIA, the National Security Administration, the Department of Defense and all the unlimited resources of the American superpower are at its disposal. Two days later, on 8 February, the Israelis announce that they will resume the hunt and offer a bounty of $1 million to whoever delivers Mengele. The rewards for his capture become astronomical: the Simon Wiesenthal Center and the *Washington Times* add a million dollars each, Germany adds a million marks . . . Forty years after the end of the war, Mengele's head is now worth $3,400,000. Americans, Israelis and West Germans coordinate their efforts and share their information. Journalists and adventurers invade Günzburg and South America; the media sensationalise the largest manhunt of the end of the twentieth century. They are hunting a ghost, not that anyone knows it yet.

Holocaust mania sweeps across the West as the 1978 four-part television mini-series *Holocaust*, starring Meryl Streep and James Woods, brings home the extermination of the Jews of Europe to millions of viewers in a way that nothing has done before. The series causes significant shock and has a tremendous emotional impact; the term 'Holocaust' becomes widespread, and camp survivors speak out at last. In Germany, the elite generation of Nazi administrators and managers has retired and the painful work of official rehabilitation of individual and collective memory can begin. For the United States, the Holocaust becomes a moral point of reference. Congress approves the building of a landmark museum in Washington; twenty-two memorials will rise throughout the country. Claude Lanzmann is finishing his epic film, *Shoah*.

This time, you must catch the monster and deliver 'the symbol of Nazi cruelty' to the courts, says the president of the court of Yad Vashem, the chief prosecutor in the Jerusalem trial of Eichmann. In recent years, the most bizarre information has circulated; the myth has grown; 'Herr Doktor' remains elusive. Even though Paraguay finally revoked his citizenship in the summer of 1979, many think he is still living there, protected by

205

President Stroessner's henchmen. In May 1985, Beate Klarsfeld stages a protest under the windows of the presidential palace in Asunción. Simon Wiesenthal claims that Mengele divides his time between Chile, Bolivia and Paraguay; Israel says he is in Uruguay. The *New York Post* has unmasked him in Westchester County, next door to an Orthodox *yeshiva*, not far from New York. He is a drug-trafficking baron operating between South America and the United States under the pseudonym 'Henrique Wollman', and was almost arrested in Miami. Fuelled by the success of the film *The Boys from Brazil*, in which Gregory Peck plays Josef Mengele the legend – the leader of a neo-Nazi conspiracy, he clones ninety-four little Adolf Hitlers in order to establish a Fourth Reich – suspicion grows that he is behind the proliferation of twins in Cândido Godói, a village in southern Brazil.

78.

In Günzburg, the cousins Karl-Heinz and Dieter are worried. The legal initiative and media storm threaten the family firm, and journalists camp in front of the factory and their home; the promised bounty could loosen the tongues of their greedy South American retainers. Their pact of silence holds for six years. After his father's death, Rolf returns to Brazil to retrieve his belongings, his correspondence and his notebooks. He pays

Bossert handsomely for his loyal service and offers the family half of the Eldorado bungalow. He gives the other half to the Stammers, who immediately sell it to Bossert. The two families vow to keep the secret of Uncle Pedro's death under wraps. The Günzburg clan has pulled together and also keeps quiet. An announcement would trigger embarrassing questions. The revelation of their unwavering support for the fugitive would be bad publicity for their multinational company. The Mengeles had relished the fruitless efforts of the survivors, governments and Nazi hunters to capture the fugitive. Rolf, in keeping with his internal contradictions, stays quiet out of loyalty to his father's allies. Although he hates his cousins, he hopes, as they do, that the remains of his father will never be discovered and that Mengele will be lost in time. Compromising witnesses have disappeared one after another: Gerhard already a while ago, Rudel and Krug in 1982.

But by the end of winter 1984, the Mengele family needs to change tactics. The pressure is too great. Articles incriminate the company, which is suspected of supplying the fugitive's Swiss bank account. In March 1985, Dieter gives an interview to a major US TV channel. He denies any contact with his uncle since his escape from Argentina; he says he assumed Josef Mengele was dead – 'men die young in the family'. If he were alive, his uncle would be seventy-four years old. Let there be no misunderstanding: he has no information. But Dieter's performance only fuels speculation: of course Mengele is alive; his nephew is scheming to throw them off the scent now that all the intelligence services and the police are on his tail. The hunt must intensify. Rolf is angry with Dieter, who did not forewarn him about the TV interview. At the end of March, the three cousins meet up in Günzburg. Dieter suggests digging up the bones in the Embu cemetery, bringing them back to Germany and dropping them at the door of the prosecutor in charge of the hunt with an anonymous note, 'Here are the remains of Josef Mengele.' Rolf refuses. He advocates absolute silence. With a little luck, the skeleton will never be found.

But the tide is turning: in autumn 1984, loyal Sedlmeier leaked some secrets during a dinner in the Black Forest where he and his wife were on holiday. It was a jolly evening and well oiled. The devil's clerk loosened up: he told a friend that he had never stopped sending money to Mengele. The man spoke to the police, who issued a mandate. On 10 May 1985, in Frankfurt, the German prosecutor informs his American and Israeli partners of a pending search at Sedlmeier's. This time, Günzburg police keep out of the way and do not warn the interested party.

At the end of the month, the police search Sedlmeier's luxurious villa. In his wife's dressing room, they seize an address book, a list of coded telephone numbers and the photocopied correspondence of Mengele, Bossert and the Stammers. One of Bossert's letters announces the death of Mengele. Sedlmeier refuses to cooperate, and he is put under house arrest while the police decrypt the address book, which leads them to Brazil. Alerted, the police of São Paulo keep the Bossert and Stammer families under surveillance for four days, 24/7. There's no sign of Mengele. On 5 June, the Bosserts' home is raided at dawn.

Junk, trinkets and recent photos of the old moustachioed man are found in a dresser and confirm the family's ties with Mengele. Bossert swiftly spills the beans: Mengele is dead and buried in Embu cemetery in a vault under the name of Wolfgang Gerhard. The following day, Gitta Stammer is more resilient: indeed she does recognise the man in the picture. It is Peter Hochbichler, the Swiss man who managed their farms for a long time. Gerhard introduced them. But she does not know any Josef Mengele. Geza is not questioned, as he is on a cruise in Asia.

The same day, on the other side of the world, there is a sensational leak to the press: five columns of page-one news in *Die Welt* announce the discovery of Mengele's corpse in Brazil. On 6 June, a forest of cameras, photographers and microphones surrounds the police and the Bosserts, who come to witness the exhumation of the contents of Gerhard's grave at Embu das Artes. The earth is excavated, the coffin hoisted up, its cover broken, and the skeleton finally laid bare. The director of the Forensic Laboratory of Police in São Paulo brandishes the skull as though he had unearthed the fossil of a mythical reptile hunted for centuries. The real face of the monster is mud coloured, teeming with worms, a vanity, the triumph of Death.

The best forensic doctors come to Brazil to identify the remains. The Israelis and the Klarsfelds are sceptical. Why was the family tight-lipped for six years? Why complicate life to such a degree? And why now? It is definitely a new smoke screen raised so that Mengele can enjoy his last years in peace.

Wiesenthal does not believe it, either: this is the seventh time the war criminal has died – once on the Russian front, twice in Paraguay, once in Brazil, another time in Bolivia, and even recently in Portugal where he is alleged to have committed suicide.

Meanwhile, the experts determine the blood group of the skeleton, recover hair from the head and moustache, take a fingerprint, measure the bones and the gap between the upper front teeth, examine the vertebrae, the femurs, a hole in the left cheekbone and the prominent forehead. They superimpose photos of Mengele young and old, consult his SS file in which a fracture of the pelvis following a motorcycle accident in Auschwitz is mentioned. Rolf decides to break his silence. Initially he envisages selling to *Stern* magazine his father's letters and notebooks and the photos that he, Rolf, took during his trip to Brazil, but then decides to donate them to *Bunte*, an illustrated print magazine. The profits from issue sales will be paid to associations of concentration-camp survivors. On the cover of the issue of 18 June, the West Germans see a ravaged Mengele in a high-collared shirt and wearing a straw hat. A special report reveals that his family knew where he was hiding and supported him financially to the end. Rolf confirms, in a brief statement, that his father died in Brazil in 1979 and expresses his deepest sympathy to the victims and their loved ones. He had not revealed the death out of consideration for the people who helped his father. He does not say a word about Josef's atrocities. Dieter, Karl-Heinz and Sedlmeier hide behind a wall of silence.

On 21 June 1985, the press is summoned to police head-quarters in São Paulo. Forensic pathologists have established to a reasonable degree of scientific certainty that the skeleton discovered in Embu is that of Josef Mengele.

79.

In 1992, DNA tests confirmed the opinion of the experts.

That same year, Germany, Israel and the United States defin-itively close the file on Mengele case. His remains are stored in a cupboard in São Paulo's Legal Medical Institute. The family does not claim his mortal remains. Mengele is deprived of a grave.

Dieter, Karl-Heinz and Sedlmeier have never been prose-cuted; neither has Rolf. In Germany the charge of aiding, abetting or counselling a wanted criminal is null and void after five years. The family firm, Mengele Agrartechnik, struggled after the revelations of June 1985. By 1991 it had only 650 employees, half as many as six years previously. The firm was sold that year. By 2011 the brand had disappeared entirely.

In 2009 Dieter and Karl-Heinz Mengele created a found-ation to help those in need in Günzburg and burnish a tarnished family name 'associated with negative things in recent years', as Dieter said in an interview for the *Augsburger Allgemeine*.

The notebooks and diaries written in exile by Josef Mengele were auctioned in the United States for $245,000 in 2011. The seller and the buyer have remained anonymous.

Rolf Mengele lives and works as a lawyer in Munich. He has taken his wife's name. In an interview with an Israeli newspaper in 2008, he asked the Jewish people not to hate him because of the crimes perpetrated by his father.

80.

Mengele's bones were bequeathed to Brazilian medicine in March 2016.

81.

His mortal remains are now in the hands of forensics students at the University of São Paulo: so ends Josef Mengele's great escape, seventy years after the war that devastated the cultivated and cosmopolitan continent of Europe. This is the story of an unscrupulous man with a small, hard soul struck down by a poisonous and deadly ideology that spread through a society weakened by the disruptions of modernity. The ambitious young doctor offered no resistance to the disease of Nazism: it preyed on his mediocre tastes, his vanity, envy and avarice, inciting him to commit monstrous crimes and to justify them. Every two or three generations, as memory fades and the last witnesses of past massacres disappear, reason is eclipsed and men return to propagate evil.

From all ill dreams defend our sight, from fears and terrors of the night.

And keep us on our guard. Be wary, man is a malleable creature, we must be wary of men.

SOURCES

This book tells the story of Josef Mengele in South America. Certain shadowy areas will probably never be illuminated. Only the genre of narrative nonfiction has allowed me to get close to the macabre journey of the Nazi doctor. I went to Günzburg, Argentina and Brazil to research this book, and visited the farm at Santa Lúci, in the region of Serra Negra. Of the many books I studied, a few have been essential to the preparation of this book. That of Miklós Nyiszli, *Auschwitz, A Doctor's Eyewitness Account* (Julliard, 1961), to begin with. I also quote from the works of Ulrich Völklein, *Josef Mengele, der Arzt von Auschwitz* (Steidl, 2003), Gerald Astor, *The Last Nazi* (Sphere Books, 1986) and Sven Keller, *Günzburg und der Fall Josef Mengele* (Oldenbourg, 2003). *Mengele, The Complete Story*, by Gerald L. Posner and John Ware (Cooper Square Press, 2000), is an unparalleled mine of information and is, in my view, the best biography of Mengele in existence. In the 1980s, Posner and Ware gained access to the diaries of the fugitive doctor. Concerning Perón's Argentina and his policy of welcoming Nazi war criminals, *La Autentica Odessa d'Uki*

Goñi (Paidos Iberica, 2002) and *Eichmann Before Jerusalem* by Bettina Stangneth (The Bodley Head, 2014) are superb. *La Loi du sang* (Gallimard, 2014) by Johann Chapoutot was invaluable for getting to grips with the Nazi worldview.

ACKNOWLEDGEMENTS

To Juliette Joste, Christophe Bataille and Olivier Nora, Marion Naccache, Juan Alberto Schulz, Uki Goñi, Sébastien Le Fol, Lars Kraume, Léa Salamé, Sylvie and Gilles Guez, Danièle Hirsch.

And to Annabelle Hirsch. Annabelle.